Dedication

    This is long for a dedication, so forgive me. First off, let me get the negative ones out of the way so we finish on a high note.

    I'd like to firstly thank my university Creative Writing class, for making me drop out of English and actually making me become more of a writer as a result. I know for sure if I'd continued with you, this project would never have come to pass. Let that be a crystalline lesson for you all – you don't need Creative Writing classes to write. This is not to say they have no merit, but that if you shackle yourself to them, then you'll write as they proscribe. Know your Creative Writing class, and then judge for yourself. I've heard nothing but positive feedback from all other years of that class, so maybe it was just not for *me*.

    I'd also like to thank Tracy, for hurting me in the worst way possible, and crippling me from writing for ten years. Without you, this world would never have reached the level of redevelopment it's seen, as I tried again and again to write, without making it anywhere. The lesson here is, you can take good out of the bad life has given you. It doesn't just have to be healing. And it sure as hell doesn't have to be forgiveness.

    Now, for the positives.

    I'd like to thank all of those who I call friend,

because you support me no matter what you think. You're there, and you support me simply by having a good day, every time. And we support each other, when we have bad days. Among these, of special note are my friend Jinx, who gave me shelter in one of the times I needed it most; my friends Alex and Kitty for giving me a place to write this story from; and my friend Chris for being a brother to me through hard times for each of us.

Secondly I'd like to thank those assembled friends who formed my beta reader group, of which I have not given an actual name. But the reading and the commentary you give shape this story as much as my hands, so it's only fair you see credit for this. Even those of you who read without commentary are of benefit, because you buffer me simply by being a willing reader.

Lastly, I'd like to thank someone who makes this possible, because she gives me the strength to finally write about this world that I've been dreaming about for eighteen long years. She gave me the strength to seek out medicinal help for my psychological problems, which include among them both bipolar disorder and ADHD. I'd like to thank her, but no thanks will *ever* be enough for what's owed her.

I love you, Fee, now, always. And thank you for being a reason I can write.

Foreword

  Where do I begin? I'll be completely honest, I wrote "Iron and Tempest" mostly for myself. Out of a desire to prove that I could, that my writing muscles weren't completely crippled, that my demons that haunt my writing senses weren't stronger than I was. And as it turns out, you know what? They weren't, on either account. Instead, here we are at the start of my first book, and what might end up being a series. I'll be honest, after "Iron and Tempest" I'm probably going to take a break, slow down for a while, see where things stand. See if people want more, see if I even feel like writing more. And if the answer to both of those is yes? Then forward we'll go, and we'll see where we end up heading. Right now? I have no plans that extend past the end of this book. I mean, I know what's going to happen, but right now, there is no plan that involves writing it.

  I'm also writing this foreword as I approach the midpoint of this book. In fact, I could even tell you what the next thing to happen will be. But I won't. Because in theory you're reading this before you read the book itself. And if not, what's wrong with you? It's a foreword. 'Fore'-word. As in, 'before'. You were supposed to read this first, since it might give you insight into what's going on. Do I think it will actually give you insight? Probably not, but you'll be more familiar with how I talk, how I do things, and maybe that alone will make some things in the book feel better, make more sense.

How did I come up with this entire world? Unsurprisingly it didn't happen overnight. This is something that's been brewing in my head for approximately eighteen years. Long enough for a human to become an adult. Older than two of our main protagonists. And it's been developed and redeveloped and redeveloped again, more times than I know of. I was just getting ready to start writing it when a personal disaster happened, and basically for ten years, I wrote nothing. Or next to nothing, nothing of any import. But I've already gone into that as much as I will, so don't worry about this turning into some sob story.

These people are not based on people I know, though I definitely borrowed characteristics from them, and from myself, to make the characters that fill this world. There are character choices I made because I want people to feel like they have at least someone they can identify with. I may not have done a perfect job, and for that I apologize in my lackluster efforts. These people are as much who you want them to be as who I want them to be. There are certain individuals who may be of an indistinct gender, or their description leads to an assumption that doesn't match the gender stated. This is also deliberate, as is the sexuality of certain characters. And also the appearance of many of the characters. I hope I did them justice, as I do not belong to all these minorities, and I wish them to be fairly seen, so that people know that *they* are seen. Please, if you feel you were not represented or kin to you were not represented, absolutely let me know. I don't expect to hit all arms of our life and society equally, nor do I expect that they'll all be included within this book itself. But I will try.

Serious stuff out of the way, another of my goals in this project is to make the concept of high fantasy approachable to the individual and specifically to those who may not normally indulge in the genre. As such, many of the characters speak colloquially compared to the high educated and informed speech you'd expect in a high fantasy. Speaking in that high-educated fashion is the abnormality, not the rule, even in places you'd expect otherwise.

Lastly, I don't expect this work to be excellent. I don't even expect it to be good. But I want it to *be*. As the wisdom of the internet told me, "You can't edit a blank page." And you can't start writing unless you start. I will gladly accept criticism, as it can only make me stronger as a writer, All that I ask is that you be fair with your criticism, and not petty, hateful, or crude.

That's all for now. I love you all, and I'll see you around some day.

Chapter 1

The stars spun idly across the sky, as uncaring of the world as they could be. But they spun idly over a world of wonders and terrors. A world that bore the scars of war and the marks of healing calm. A world that once saw the footprints of gods and mortals side by side. A world that even now, has its struggles and its blessings.

They spun above a husband and his wife out in a fishing boat, lazing away the evening while catching the next day's lunch. They spun above a man dressed in ivory and scarlet colours, alone in a large marble room, empty save for an extravagant throne and scarlet carpet streaking down the centre of the room. They spun above a man in an underground chamber, sleepless and stained with the detritus of effort and combat. And they spun above a child who slept soundly, guarded by a vigilant mother against the terrors of the night.

***

Tyrielle stretched her right hand carefully. Seventeen years and the burns stilled ached as freshly as the days afterwards that they had healed. They did not impede her much, not anymore, but in the early days she remembered being nearly incapacitated from the pain and the damage from the burning. The only reason she escaped was her husband's brother Zarik leading them away from the conflagration that consumed their new home and her husband Myr.

Myr... not a day went by that she did not miss him, even seventeen years later. Not even for solace or the comfort of a warm body had she taken anyone to bed – not that the callers were falling over themselves to grab her attention. Not anymore. A middling-to-elderly aged woman, with a burn that covered half her face and most of the right side of her body was not exactly the catch that suitors were looking for these days, if ever.

The pain from her hand brought her attention back to the present. She wrapped her fingers around the hilt of her sword – not the sword she bore in her service days, but a reliable, trusty short sword, one that did not stand out, that would not identify her to anyone as a person of interest. But a sword that was still far more than serviceable for her needs.

She looked out the door's window, to the

evening - leading towards night - sky. She looked up and saw the stars beginning to come out. Like she had for two dozen years, she lifted the silver pendant of a hollow circle and kissed it before tucking it back inside her shirt. The pendant was a gift from Myr early on into their courtship, a gift from the intellectual-looking man of a family of mages to the militant daughter of a militant family.

    That thought, combined with a soft chirp of a snore, caused Tyrielle to look behind her into the room. Arzades slept soundly on the single mattress inside the room, content to rest while Tyrielle watched. A routine that they had followed for sixteen years, Arzades would sleep while Tyrielle kept watch throughout the night. And in the earlier days, it was hard, because she would need to be awake during the day to take care of him then, as well.

    Tyrielle shook her head to clear the intrusive thoughts. There would be time enough for those when Arzades was grown up and able to take care of himself. He would be either a truly great and powerful mage like his father, or a practiced swordsman like his mother. Either way, his path was clear to care for himself; Tyrielle just needed to make sure he would get there. In seventeen years, there was no sign of anyone following, or hunting, or tracking them. But her enemies were clever, calculating, things that she was no stranger to.

    This house, the first real one that Arzades had to call home, stood a day's march east from the nearest village, a place called Arvil, and they would travel that far only rarely. In the intervening years, Tyrielle had learned many trades to help disguise her presence amidst the common people of the Crosslands. These days, she considered herself a hunter and a farmer – tending crops by day, hunting on occasion into the evening, and watching over her son at night. Arzades helped out with the crops now, but spent a great deal of his time daydreaming about life outside the small, constrained bubble that she kept them both inside.

Thinking now of Arzades' daydreaming, she looked down at her right hand again. Someday he would be a powerful mage, but only if he received the teachings necessary. She found his power manifesting in a dozen small ways, tricks to follow his dreams and whims. Otherwise, if Myr was right, Arzades would merely be a boiling pot held under pressure, spraying out steam and sizzling water, whenever he was under stress or excited. There would be no telling the damage he could cause, and she was woefully unprepared to deal with the consequences. Only a mage could teach a mage, and while she knew *where* she could go for his teaching, she only knew one mage other than Myr. And he would see her and her son dead as soon as they presented themselves to his sight.

Once more she found herself shaking her head to clear it physically of the mental intrusions. She scanned the treeline, the skies, and, seeing nothing, returned her gaze to her son. "Tomorrow," she thought, "tomorrow I'll begin teaching him to defend himself." That thought in mind, she set foot outside the home and began wandering the fields and treeline searching for suitable tools. Sticks of a proper length to start with. Once she collected a number of sticks that matched her criteria, she turned to home and sat outside on the rocking chair. A chair which her sole friend in the village of Arvil, Renias, a blacksmith - and amateur woodcarver and carpenter by his own admission - had made.

    She began shearing off the twigs with a knife - except where they might present themselves as a crossguard - and laid them aside to continue on with the next one. In the monotony, her mind slipped away once more, but not to Myr or Arzades, but instead her father, the great Lord General, the man who taught her to fight. Taught her to fight by giving her a sword and open-hand slapping it away, or slapping her, with every failed attempt she launched.

    She remembered nearly every blow she suffered under his tutelage and anger began suffusing her, the whittling of the sticks becoming more energetic and dedicated as she remembered. It was only weeks that passed before she began striking her father with some degree of regularity, and that was when things changed. He took their family sword off the wall and faced off with her, wielding it, where she only had a simple, common, short blade. Not too dissimilar from the one she bore in current days, in fact, but still one that left her at a vast disadvantage due to the difference in reach and quality.

She remembered the day that she won the fight in her eyes, before he cheated. It started with a rapid exchange of blows, a quick probing to see if either was leaving a gap in their defenses, before it settled down into pacing back and forth. Careful eyes watching each other, her hazel versus his brown. She launched a probing attack now and then, she noticed it. His left side was just a fraction of a second slower to defend. She began sliding that way consistently, forcing him to turn, forcing him to defend on that side where she had an advantage. A last rapid exchange of blows, and he found himself with a cut forearm and a disarmed weapon before his daughter. Tyrielle remembered the feeling of pride at having won a duel, finally, with the old man, when he *unthinkably* kicked her square in the chest, more than hard enough to knock the wind out of her – he even cracked ribs with that blow. And before she could recover, she felt the tip of his blade at her neck. Words were spoken that burned themselves into her mind and heart then. "Just because an enemy is defeated, doesn't mean they're harmless."

That was the last day they fought. After that she endured training of various physical kinds. A teacher for weaponless combat. A dancing instructor. A fencing tutor that became more like a bodyguard and friend to her. A circus acrobat. All these and more she endured to become the person she was, the former champion of the Empire of the West. Once she held that title, only then did her father begin treating her with a modicum of respect. Only then did he take her into his study, and they began discussing military strategy on a grander scale than the dueling combat she had become accustomed to. From the squadron level to the army level, they would discuss, he would quiz, and she would answer. Some answers earned a frown, some bore no change in expression, and the rare one would earn an eyebrow raise and a, "Not bad," from him.

    Tyrielle looked down at the current stick, whittled into a small wooden stake and smiled, tossing it aside and lifting the next one. Not all memories are bad, she reminded herself, and began whittling the next stick she would use, likely, to thrash her son tomorrow.

Chapter 2

Renias pulled the boat into the small docks attached to their home. His wife, Alari, tied off the boat quickly with practiced ease as he lifted the small basket of fish they had procured. Together they walked into the house and began preparing the fish, scaling the fish and filleting the flesh free before storing them in the small, modest cellar they had, inside a salt room. They did not properly salt or otherwise preserve the fish, as these were for tomorrow's meal when their children would be over to visit. But it was still the chilliest room inside their small house.

Alari shooed Renias out of the house while she continued preparations, so Renias sat on the front doorstep, smoking from a pipe he had crafted himself, congratulating himself on a successful day of fishing. Fishing was always a chancey endeavour you see, since one day, a spot could prove lucrative, and the next, dry as a desert. So he celebrated every time he was successful in catching something.

Beside the house, the forge sat empty, down to embers in the chamber and tools all hung in their assigned place. He worked purely off of commissions; since the village was so small, there was not much point in keeping extra stock around. Sure, from time to time he would feel the urge to just create something, but besides that, he kept the forge itself going, but low to embers, so that if the time came for him to work on an order, it would not take him ages of clearing the ash and soot from the chamber before laying new wood and coal and lighting it.

Renias tapped the pipe empty and stood up. Inside, Alari was cleaning and organizing the house to be ready for guests such as they would have tomorrow. Indeed, she had shooed Renias outside in order for her to be able to work to her satisfaction, to which Renias had no problem. He looked down the sole street of the village to the headman's house, the place that served as a communal drinking hall, and set off whistling down the street.

The houses he passed were unremarkable to most, but he helped build many of them, or rebuild them, or remodel them at the very least. He could name the owners of each house as he passed. He passed by the house of his son, Marik, and smiled that way, seeing the light still vaguely visible inside. He made it to the house of the headman, a veritable mansion by the standards of Arvil. Walking around to the side of the house where the town stables were also kept, he stepped inside the shelter afforded to the animals to a chorus of hushed greetings from the gathered villagers there. Marik was there, as was the headman's son Terth, with Renias' own daughter, Eillel. All the villagers he expected to see were there. But then he saw the cause for the curbed enthusiasm. There was a stranger, looked fairly young from his appearance and well off, but alone. He sat nursing a drink at the roughly shaped bar and barely lifted his head to acknowledge Renias' entrance. He was also armed, a long slender blade at his side, a piece of beauty.

Renias moved to join his children and the headman's son at their chosen table and poured himself an extra mug of ale from the pitcher on the table. With a wink to his daughter, he promised to drink her share as well, before downing half the mug in a single go.

"Who's the new guy?" he finally asked to a chorus of shrugs and murmured half-responses from his tablemates. Shrugging back, he continued to nurse the ale, soaking in the low conversation and the close camaraderie of the village drinking hall, impacted only slightly by the stranger.

Perhaps an hour, maybe two, later, Renias

stopped before pouring himself a third round of ale. An itch on the back of his neck warned him off it, warned him that his wits might need to be called upon. But he remained for some time yet, chatting with the others, talking to other villagers as they came and presented themselves. Even took an order for nails from one of the farmers who had come in to drink. Deciding that Alari had had enough time to clean and reorganize the house, Renias stood up to leave, stepping out from the eaves of the stable, and started to walk his way home.

"Blacksmith," called out a smooth voice, prompting him to turn back. It was the stranger. "I've already asked the headman, who told me nothing of what I seek. I figured as smiths are important the more remote a village is, you might be the next best person to consult, so I asked and your friends told me who you were. I'm looking for someone. A woman, in her middle years, probably strict in her speech and bearing. Likely armed. Silvery hair before her time. Likely with burns down her side," the young man rattled off, and Renias' mind clicked. He knew exactly who this young man was looking for. And if he was here, chances were reasonable that the stranger knew Tyrielle was here as well; it was just a matter of time.

"Yeah, I know the lady you're looking for. She's got a kid with her, maybe a bit younger than you," he replied, probing to see how much the man knew. A look of brief surprise on his face told

Renias much, that he did not know about the existence of Arzades, and that it was definitely Tyrielle he was looking for. "What's it to you?"

"I've been...conscripted to find her. That's all I will say. Where does the lady live?"

"She comes in from outside town somewhere. I ain't been to her home."

"Then, where does she come in from at the very least? I will seek her out myself if need be."

Renias' mind whirred with possibilities. Should he deceive the young man and be found out, he was ill-equipped to face a swordsman. Should he not, he would be setting an unknown on Tyrielle without warning, and that was something he found unconscionable. So, he took a breath. "She comes in from the south, e'ery time I've seen her come in."

The man paused for a moment, then nodded. "Then tomorrow I leave for the south and start searching for her. Do you have any advice for directions?"

"No, young sir. I don't leave the village much except for fishing, and I can tell you she don't live on the water."

"Fishing, eh? I'm not a bad hand at fishing myself. Though I've fished on the open expanse of the Emeraldsea, not on small backwoods lakes and rivers."

Renias paused for a moment, choosing his words carefully. "I've heard fishing on the open sea is far more exciting, where small river fishing is a game of patience and dedication, compared to the ocean's wildness."

The young man nodded, leaning against a post of the stables, backlit by lantern light so that Renias could not see his face. "It's indeed exciting and a test of strength and will. My father told me that a patient man fishes in the small, quiet places of the world, but it takes a wild man to fish on the open seas. I take it you've not been on the open seas much if at all, then?"

"No, young sir. I haven't been away from the village since I moved here, forge and all. Too heavy to put it on a boat like that."

The young man chuckled at that and waved Renias off. "Thank you for your time, blacksmith. I'm going to get another drink and see about a room with someone. Sleep you well," he said before turning back inside and returning to the bar for his drink.

Renias turned to head back to his home, struggling not to move with a hurried step, to remain calm and collected. Once home, he took deep breaths before looking up to Alari. "I won't be home for dinner tomorrow, my heart. There's a stranger in town looking for Tyrielle, and I have to warn her. I misdirected him off to the south, but there's no telling how long it'll be before he realizes the trick."

Alari simply nodded and grabbed a pack from a nearby shelf, shoving some sweetmeats, jerky, and hardtack into the leather satchel. "I'll make sure you're ready to leave tomorrow as soon as you wake up, Renias. Go to sleep. I'll take care of everything else."

Renias shook his head and moved over to beside Alari. "I can take care of that myself, it's the least I can do, dear heart. I suspect that she'll be wanting to see this newcomer for herself, but I can't say for sure. So best get ready for different guests in a couple days from now, while I start taking care of this, then call it an early night," he said calmly, lifting the bag from her grip and kissing her hand before she released the satchel.

Alari smiled at her husband, caressing his cheek before she turned and started counting out what she would need for a meal for four people in a couple days, combined with the meal for her son and his wife tomorrow while Renias was gone. Sighing, she resigned herself to fishing tomorrow as well, before she needed to be back for dinner preparations. She would need to head to bed early herself.

After filling the bag with assorted dried goods that would sustain him on the day long trip, Renias stepped into the only other room their small house held, a small but well-appointed bedroom. Stripping his smock off and laying in bed, he stared out the window at the stars that whirled overhead. Shortly after, he was joined by Alari who wordlessly sunk herself into his side and closed her eyes.

"Tomorrow, east, Tyrielle and her boy, and then we'll see what's next," he murmured to himself and the rafters of his small home that suddenly felt closed and oppressive.

Chapter 3

Morning came, and with that, Tyrielle roused Arzades from his sleep and, before she took her own sleep, she beckoned him forward for a quick conversation. "Today I'm going to start teaching you how to fight.

Arzades leaned forward, keenly interested and his attention piqued by his mother's opening declaration. "Are you sure? I mean, of course I'm interested, but you've always turned me down before," he replied, brushing a hand over his chin, before leaning back against the wall by the door.

"Well, for one, you wanted it too much, pup. But now, you're more physically fit for it, you're less likely to damage your growth permanently. I plan on making you capable enough to take care of yourself before the year is out, and this is the way I know. Were I a mage like your father, or knew a mage, we'd cover those topics instead, But, we don't, and I don't. So we're going about this the hard way. And," she said, pausing, smirking ruefully before continuing, "I'm starting to get old, too old to always be taking care of you."

"*Starting* to get old?"

Arzades did not see his mother pick up the knife from its hanging spot on the wall, nor did he see it move through the air. But he did feel the razor's edge tug at the hair on the side of his head. He exhaled noisily through his nose before reaching up and pulling the knife free. He moved across the room to look his mother in the hazel eyes, before reaching over and hanging the knife back in its place. "Yes, starting to get old, you brat," she corrected through smirking lips, reaching up and patting Arzades' cheek with a cupped hand, "So, what I want you to do is this. I'm going to catch some sleep. I want you to take your normal route for your hike today, but the stretch from the last tree to here, I want you to take at a full sprint. After that, I want you to stretch your muscles, as near to all of them, as you can. Then, wake me up – don't worry, pup, I'll doze throughout the rest of the day, – and we'll repeat those stretches. Anything else can wait until I'm awake. Understand?"

He nodded in response, and Tyrielle went to the bed, stripping down and leaning her sword against the wall before taking her place and beginning the process of dozing off, leaving Arzades to his own devices. Were he more mischievous or of a similar attitude, perhaps he might have retaliated on his mother. But instead he left the small house to take in the fresh air. Noticing the small pile of sticks, he took one in hand and swished it around in the air, like a tyke would with any wooden sword. Satisfied with himself, he carried it with him and set off on a walk. Before any thoughts of his hike, it was his task today to make sure the crops were tended to. A simple enough task.

One that availed Arzades of a lot of time to daydream.

His life was a closed, confined field of next to no excitement. His mother always said that was the point, but you can ask any adolescent anywhere, and they will tell you the same thing; they are bored and want something to happen. Arzades was no different. While detasseling the corn, he was imagining being the loyal and subservient knight to a beautiful princess. Fighting monsters, demons, dragons, foul conjurations and terrible aberrations; he took it all on for his beloved Princess. While weeding the root vegetables, he was a wise and venerable sagely wizard who could lift mountains with his mind, part the Emeraldsea to walk across the bottom, and conjure blasts of flame into the air around him. Were he paying more attention, he might have noticed curious things happening around him. He might have noticed the smaller of the rocks next to him lifting on end and spinning into the air and floating. He might have noticed that within the small irrigation channel that his mother and Renias had dug into the ground, the water diverted, slid up and out of the channel and spilled across the ground itself. And, lastly, he might have noticed the grass nearby curling and crisping as if under the weight of a tremendous heat.

But he did not, he daydreamed on as he tended the crops.

***

An hour and some later, he grabbed a small sack full of trail snacks and his selected stick, and took off on his hike. He generally followed a trail he had laid out, one that surveyed a number of chosen landmarks and features, and today was no different. The first stop along his trek was a forest pond from which he often found various wildlife drinking fearlessly, where he could join them on a nearby rock and watch. In his time there, he watched several deer come to the pool and drink. They would turn to watch him carefully as they approached the pool, drink their fill, and then swiftly leave. Even a great brown bear came to the pool and drank its fill. That one came over to Arzades and snuffled at the base of the rock before turning away. Arzades released a held breath and crawled on down from the rock, deciding not to press his luck, and continued forward with his trek. The next stop was his favourite one. A place he had taken his mother to see a couple years ago, that he called Phoenix Rock.

It started as always with a climb. But the footholds and handholds were so familiar to him, he could climb them in his sleep. Indeed, out of curiosity, he tried one day to climb blindfolded, and made it up to all but the last stretch. The cracked rock made for easy climbing, and the red stone spread wide gave Arzades the inspiration for it's name. He passed the first two places for sitting that he had accustomed to and sat on the third, a small stretch of stone large enough for him to stretch out but no more, and looked out east across the forest. He had only heard tales of the Emeraldsea, stories of his mother's and once of a traveling bard's while they were in a village, while they were traveling still. To him, the dark and light greens that blended together to form this nameless forest, this was *his* Emeraldsea. He thought they must look much the same after all, between stories of his mother's about the sea and the eponymous gem.

Shaking his head for a moment, a twitch he had learned from his mother, he stood and lifted the stick he looted from the supply his mother assembled. Imagining it as a sword, different from his mother's, he imagined it a longer, slender blade, laden with golden trim and gems along its hilt and pommel. Smiling, he practiced similar strokes to the ones he tested the stick out with, and before long, he started taking steps side to side, back and forth, feet skittering across the uneven rock. More than once he came close to stepping straight off the edge of the rock into an easy ten metre drop. But the adrenaline just drove him into more furious and flurrying blows, thrashing the air with his imagined blade, felling foes in droves as they presented themselves to his steel.

He paused to take a breath and calmed himself down from his flurry and closed his eyes. He pictured his mother, in her fighting leathers, with her sword. Envisioned the poses she took, the movements she invoked and the forms she moved through. Slowly the movements became more and more fluid, and something in Arzades spoke to him, that he was ready to learn what his mother had to teach him directly, that he had learned all he could just by watching. Thrusting the stick through a belt-loop, he gathered his supplies and climbed back down the rock and patted the side of it, smiling warmly.

The last stop he had was one that his mother had put there. Arzades never knew his father, and from what his mother said, there was next to no chance that they would ever find the legitimate resting place of his body. But they found a small rock and Tyrielle over the course of days carved into it the name and the details that would be found on a resting stone. And Arzades helped her place it at the base of the greatest tree within a day's walk of their home. Every time he went on his hike, he would stop by and care for the memorial, from time to time noticing signs that his mother had been there, but mostly alone. That was the way – his mother rarely showed any release of emotion, especially not one as intense as grief.

Sighing, he sat down beside the stone, resting a hand on its face, tracing the words and speaking them aloud. "Myr Anderwyn. Mage. Devoted husband, posthumous father. Champion of a cause that never took flight."

"Father... dad... I'm learning how to fight today. If mother tells me right, you never learned how, so I suppose that's one way I'm surpassing you. That's what every parent wants, right? Their child to grow up to be... more than they are. If I'm a mage, then it's news to me. But mother says I'd need a teacher in order to really manifest anything serious in the way of powers. And that if I'm to stay safe, I may never be able to find a teacher."

"Father... why did you have to die? You left mother and I alone. I know I've asked this before, if not every time I stop here to visit you, but I never get an answer. I don't expect one, not really, but I hope in asking, that maybe someday I can answer it for myself. But it hasn't happened yet. I still have no clue. Why couldn't you protect us *and* run from whatever danger it is that you and mother faced? She's never told me what, saying that knowing wouldn't help me cope with it at all, would only cause me more feelings of hopelessness and helplessness. But I have to say, it feels pretty damned hopeless and helpless not knowing at all," Arzades spoke as he sat by the memorial stone for a while.

"Father... one more thing before I go. Do you think mother will be surprised if I know more than she thinks I should know? For fighting, I mean. Everything else is another question. I'm sure she expects me to know more about these woods than her, after all. I hope so. I hope I can see the look of surprise on her face as I land a hit or two before she expects it."

Arzades leaned over and, brushing the top of the stone clear, pressed his lips to it in a kiss before patting the stone. "Great talk as always, dad. I'll talk to you later." With that, he set foot towards the edge of the clearing, pausing briefly to take in the wind, the feeling of the air moving around him, imagining the embrace of a man he never knew, before he began the last leg of the journey home.

As he came over the crest of the hill behind the house, he looked down to the house and saw that his mother was awake and was talking with someone, who resembled Renias, the smith from town that was friends and a helper to his mother. They turned towards him as he started coming down the hill, waiting for him before speaking again, all thoughts of his mother's instruction gone from his mind.

Chapter 4

Tyrielle waited for Arzades to trail his way down the hill towards home. Comfortable in the presence of Renias, she was nonetheless both tired and distressed. The news he brought was discomfiting at best, but it made no sense. But she wanted to wait for Arzades before talking that over; he was old enough now to partake in discussions like that. And she wanted Renias there for any more details about this young man that was so interested in her whereabouts.

As Arzades approached, she noted a couple of things; he was carrying one of the sticks she had trimmed in preparation for later today – not that teaching Arzades how to fight was necessarily still on the agenda for today, but depending on the outcome of the discussion between the three - and he was bearing a grim, serious expression that told her he must have stopped by the memorial again. She sighed and nodded to him as he approached.

"Renias. What's the special occasion?" he called out as he got closer, tossing the stick back into the pile of other sticks, laying aside the small satchel he had brought along for food on his trek.

"News from the village, pup. Renias?" she gestured to the blacksmith, who sighed before beginning to speak. "So, last night there was a stranger, a kid or young man, rather, about the same age as your boy, in the village drinking hall. Not totally unusual, we're not too far off a big road for all that, but he did catch up to me on my way home asking about your mother. He didn't know about you, nor did he know where exactly you were. I sent him off south of town to buy time for your mother to decide what to do."

"That's odd, isn't it mother? If it was something dangerous, wouldn't it be more than one - and young at that - man?"

"That's exactly my thought, pup. All the same, I think it's best if we know as much as possible about this young man. Renias?"

"He was about the same height as your boy, and if I had to guess, about the same age too."

"See? I told you I was a young man, mother, not -"

"Don't interrupt, Arzades."

"Err, yes, mother, of course."

"As I was saying, he had a dark colouring to

his hair, freckles and acne marks across his face, and green eyes."

"Sounds like someone from the Empire's coast of the Emeraldsea, then. I don't know anyone who's a friend there, but the few people who survived the rebellion scattered to the winds – even Zarik abandoned me once we crossed the border into the Crosslands. Anything else, Renias?"

"He was also carrying a sword. A longer, slender blade. If I had to guess, a fencer's blade of some kind, something beyond my experience however. He also talked to me about fishing on the open seas versus fishing on quiet backwater lakes and rivers, but I suspect that's less useful."

"The more we know the better an idea we have of who this person is. Arzades, what do you think?"

Arzades paused to consider the question. He knew his mother did not ask it idly, so this was likely some kind of test she wanted to put to him, so he gave it serious thought. "If I had to say, I don't think he's an enemy. I don't know if he's a friend, though, and we don't know if he was followed by someone who is very definitely *not* a friend. In the end, I think we should meet him cautiously and maybe take some kind of measure of him before we decide one way or the other."

Tyrielle nodded in response, unsurprised by his insights – daydreamer and idler he might be, she was well aware that he was not slow or incompetent of thought. "Probably a very wise suggestion. To that end, I think we'll be going back into the village with you, Renias. Here's my plan: Arzades, you'll hang out in the drinking hall, waiting for him to come back. Renias, if you're willing, I'd like you to be there too. When he comes back, he'll probably confront you about the misdirection, and Arzades, I want you to intervene on his behalf – I leave it up to you as to how."

"Of course. Does that mean you're not going to teach me how to fight today?"

"Oh, you're not getting out of it that easily. Renias, you can go ahead and head back home after you've taken a break here if you like. You look like you could use it at the very least. I know for sure that I certainly could. But, tired or not, I've got a pup to thrash today," she said, smirking with the last minute change of heart, her face refusing to contort into the smirk due to the burns. She reached down to the pile of sticks and selected one for herself and then she paused, considering options. After a moment, she picked up the stick Arzades had pulled for himself and tossed it back to him, and stepped off the front porch into the clearing between the house and the cornstalks. Arzades followed her out carefully, stick held low in front of him like he saw her carry hers, feet moving in slow, careful motions, barely leaving the ground if at all.

Tyrielle looked her son up and down and nodded approvingly. "This won't take as long as I thought, you've already got the most basic principles down, how to move and how to keep your feet. But we'll see where you really need work after a few bouts. So come on, pup, take that stick in your hand and try to touch me with it."

Renias had since moved to the rocking chair of Tyrielle's and taken his seat to watch the exchange between the mother and son. He had never seen either of them fight at all, but he knew a swordsman's bearing when he saw it, and, between the young man from last night and the two before him right now, all three shared certain traits. But the truly worrying one to him was Tyrielle. Of the three, she was the only one he had seen capable of being completely, utterly still. Indeed, she was the only person he had *ever* seen manage that trick. Everyone had their small fidgets, worries, twitches, tics, and any of the million small involuntary movements that were natural to the body.

But Tyrielle was statuesque in her pose. Were he inclined to the artistic, he would undoubtedly try to make a sculpture from her pose right now, albeit with something perhaps a bit more heroic than a stick in hand. By comparison, Arzades was a study in careful motion. He approached his mother with one careful step after another, each step taking him further to her right side, the burned side. On the third sliding step, he launched himself forward and to the left, swinging the stick in an arc on his left. Clever of him to take advantage of the physical weakness of his mother.

Of course, it would have been more impressive if he had not ended up face down in the dirt as a result. Renias was focused more on Arzades, but he still caught the subtle motion away from the stick and the foot stuck out as Arzades' momentum carried him first past his mother, then down to the ground as a result.

Tyrielle crouched down beside her son. "You moved smartly at first, moved like you knew what you were doing, but you threw it all away when you actually went to make your attack. Additionally, you assumed that moving to my right would give you a definite advantage without probing and testing for it first. Both are why you're now on the ground. So get up, and try again," she said, moving apart and back to the spot where Arzades had started, waiting for her son's next attempt.

Arzades breathed deeply of the dust and scent of grass on the ground, coughing as the dust choked him slightly, before pushing himself up and turning back to his mother. Holding his left hand at his side, he assumed the pose he saw her start her exercises with every time, earning a cocked head from his mother. "So that's why you already know the basics, you've been stealing them by watching me," she called out, smiling before assuming the same stance.

This time, when Arzades slid forward, Tyrielle launched herself into an attack, a flurry of blows attacking mostly the stick but also Arzades' right forearm and hand. After mere moments of trying to sustain some form of defense, the stick fell from a mostly nerveless hand. "Second lesson, don't assume the enemy is going to wait for you every time."

Reaching down, Arzades flexed his hand before picking up the stick again, pushing himself up with both hands and turning to face his mother again, who was once more in a ready stance. He closed his eyes and breathed in deeply for a moment before opening them and skittering forward rapidly, launching a lunge at his mother that was easily batted aside. Then, an exchange of blows, sword to sword as it were, before Arzades played his hand and swept his left hand into the air, aiming for his mother's face and releasing the handful of dust and gravel he had grabbed earlier. She flinched and back stepped, launching a frenzied defense as she tried to clear her gaze, but Arzades pressed the attack, continuing to push her further back, until one of his strikes finally hit home, lashing into Tyrielle's side with a loud crack noise.

Renias applauded softly at that, eliciting a small bow from Arzades and a sweeping gesture before he turned back to his mother, to find her once more in a ready stance. "Good lesson, pup. Never assume your enemy will attack you with the weapon you can see. Now, let's see if you can repeat that without a trick to play," she said.

***

Hours later, Renias had since left to return

back to the village, while Arzades and Tyrielle would be leaving the next day. All day, Arzades strived to crack his mother's defense, but the dust trick was the only time he did. All too often for his tastes, the bouts ended with him on the ground, or him retrieving the stick. Once he was forced to select a new stick, as in the midst of a frenzied attack, his stick snapped just above where he gripped it. But not once did his mother let up on him. Every time he failed, she would tell him what he did wrong, and they would try again. He would repeat mistakes and curse himself for that, but they happened rarer and rarer as the day progressed.

Turning to assume a ready stance once more, he found his mother had tossed aside her stick and moved to the chair on the porch, taking a seat and beckoning Arzades forward. "Keep the sticks with you, even as we travel to the village. Become familiar with them. Since we might not be returning home from the village, make sure to grab anything else you care for before we leave. But every night from now until I tell you to stop, you'll practice with one of those sticks, basic slashes and thrust attacks. If we're near a tree, you'll use it as a practice dummy. And one more thing. If we get into an actual fight with blades drawn, if you're armed, then stand and try to take on your foe. You're already better than most who carry a sword. Remember two simple things; groin and throat. If you can save your own while slashing through your opponent's, the fight is yours. Everything else is negotiable. If you're unarmed? Run until you are," she spoke, with all the passion of a teacher repeating a lesson for maybe the hundredth time.

Arzades nodded and set foot inside the house. It struck him then how little they actually owned. A handful of woodcarvings made by each of them. Tyrielle's sword. A smattering of furniture: table and three chairs and the bed. A pair of books that Tyrielle used to teach him how to read: one on military strategy, the other a collection of children's fables that his mother read to him at night when he was younger. Maybe the knife; that'd be smart to bring along.

"Mother, I honestly don't think there's anything here I care to bring with us. The two books, maybe, but nothing else that really matters is here. Except your knife," he called out, hearing an affirmative grunt from his mother in return. Sitting on the edge of the bed, he took off his boots and laid down, staring at the ceiling. Sleep came quickly enough, with him as physically exhausted as he was, and his mother watched over outside, dozing occasionally in the comfort of the rocking chair.

Chapter 5

The next day's trek to Arvil passed mostly uneventfully. Arzades would take a stick, level it and swipe at some of the greenery they passed, beheading his 'enemies'. Tyrielle watched on with her half-smirk, and then they would keep on travelling. Every break they took from walking, Tyrielle would take a stick herself and proceed to square off against Arzades, every match telling him what he did wrong. So rapidly he was learning the craft, she found herself having to repeat lessons less often. By her figuring, as long as he kept up practicing, he would know as much as he could before facing a real opponent.

She would also have to get him a real sword soon, she realized, and half-pursed her lips thoughtfully. Maybe she could convince Renias to make something serviceable, as efficiency could be of the greatest import right now. It struck Tyrielle then that she had not the faintest idea how long it took to make a sword. She assumed it was simple, that they would have the time to wait for it, a day or two at worst. If not, they would have to get something for him before they travelled too far – Tyrielle had a feeling that they would not be returning home after meeting with this young man, regardless of what he turned out to be. The only difference would be whether or not they left a body behind them.

Hearing a cracking sound, she looked over to see Arzades chucking the remnants of another stick into the grove they had picked as a resting point. Shaking her head, she moved over to him, taking his right hand in both of hers.

"While it can be important to use all your strength to overwhelm an enemy, it is far more likely you'll need to perfect what my teacher called the 'economy of effort'. It takes very little pressure to actually cut a person," she explained, then released his hand, drew her short blade, illustrating her point by gently resting her arm on the point and gradually pressing down, ceasing when the blood began to drip down the blade. As Arzades nodded in receipt of the lesson, Tyrielle cleaned off the blade and applied pressure to the small wound, before speaking again. "What I want you to practice with your slash and thrust attacks when we have a tree for you to practice on, is to attack and stop your blade as close to the target without touching as possible. This will work on your control and accuracy while still improving your strikes," she explained, stepping back. "Anyways, pup, time to keep on moving."

She looked off wistfully to the north, noting by the position of the hills and position of the river, that they had passed where Myr's memorial was. She would have to pass by on their way away from Arvil, taking a detour if necessary, or more hopefully, passing it on the way. It was not too much further to the south before you started running into the swamps of the Marsh Realm, and there was no real purpose in traveling that direction – if this young man was an enemy, then their enemies had penetrated one country and could just as easily investigate within another. If he was not an enemy, then Tyrielle simply had no allies to speak of in the Marsh Realm, so there would be no aid for them there beyond the same small village kindness the villagers of Arvil showed when she arrived with a young, infantile Arzades in tow.

No, north would be the direction they traveled from Arvil. Perhaps they could find another small town to settle in. Maybe even apprentice Arzades to a craft to keep him out of trouble during the day. She found herself enjoying the life of a hunter and woodswoman herself, but it was not something she wanted to force on her son, as much as he was already suited towards it. Maybe they would even visit the Free Cities, sink into obscurity in the midst of a wealth of people, instead of hiding away from people altogether.

Over the hills before them, Tyrielle could see the smoke from the village fires, and she called out to Arzades that they were drawing close. He nodded and stopped his slashing and hacking with the sticks and bundled them up, tying them to his back for now.

***

Renias sat on his dock over the river, idly fishing. Alari was inside, preparing a meal for four, as they expected to see Tyrielle and Arzades soon. Even when he did feel nibbles at his bait, he was not interested in pulling the fish in. It was more just an excuse to be outside, waiting for the travellers when they got in. In the distance, he could see a pair of figures crest over the hills east of the village. Assuming their identities, he stood up and went into the house, informing, "Alari, our dinner guests will be here soon. I can see them on the hills."

Renias waited and watched his wife continue the process of cooking up fish she had caught while he was gone the previous day. She slid a rack into their oven he had built himself and dropped the sides of fish on it, reaching in with delicate tongs and turning the fish as she judged fit. "Thank you, now get out of my kitchen, you big oaf," she replied, threatening Renias mockingly with a filleting knife. Chuckling, which earned a snap of the tongs from her other hand in his direction, he went back outside.

As the two figures drew closer, he moved to the south where the small, rickety bridge over the river was. Now, it was the headman's responsibility to repair the bridge, but he just never seemed to get around to it. Always had time for drinking with the villagers though.

"Ah well. No-one's perfect," Renias muttered to himself as he lifted his arm in greeting to the pair as they drew closer and confirmed who they were.

A few minutes later, they crossed the bridge, one at a time for safety's sake, and the bridge did not crumble – yet, Renias thought, shaking his head. "Come on. Alari's seasoned and cooked up some river fish for us," he greeted them with.

"Excellent. I don't know about you, but I'm famished," Tyrielle proclaimed, moving to follow Renias as he led them back to the forge and house attached to it. Arzades paused briefly in the forge itself, touching some of the tools, before he shook himself from the reverie.

Inside, the three sat at the table while Alari continued to prepare the fish. "So, are we proceeding with the same plan you came up with?" Renias asked, earning a nod from Tyrielle.

"It's likely that he'll return either tonight or tomorrow – if he takes more than today, is it okay if we bunk here for however long it takes?" she asked. Renias turned to look at Alari who looked back and nodded. "Won't be comfortable – we sent the spare furniture off with the kids when they left home. But we can probably put together something like a bedroll with what we've got," he said, face locked in a thoughtful expression. Alari proffered plates to the seated, placing one on the table for herself as well.

"That's fine, comfort isn't of any concern to me, and Arzades can take a little bit of rough living," she quipped, earning a snort from her son directly.

"Then it'll be fine here. Anyways, let's dig into the food, and then we can go drinking," Renias replied. Arzades perked up at that, which earned a raised eyebrow from Tyrielle and her son deflated. "I guess I won't be drinking, then," he said.

"That's okay, son. I'll drink enough for the both of us."

Alari chose that moment to return with the cooked fish and some cooked root vegetables and the table was silent mostly except for the sound of eating. After a few moments passed, they pushed their plates together and Alari shooed them away, taking the plates out back and down to the dock to wash. Renias looked to Arzades and clapped him on the back. "Well, shall we, kid?" he said, standing up to leave. Arzades nodded and stood up to follow.

***

Tyrielle watched the two of them leave, head down the street, and enter into the stables that served as the drinking hall. She trusted Renias to take care of Arzades, and trusted Arzades to stop anything that might happen to Renias, before she got there at least. She left the blacksmith's house and followed afterwards down the street, finding herself a vantage point where she could see to the village's south and still see the entrance to the drinking hall.

Hours passed and it grew dark, too dark to see much outside the few torches put up around the village and the bright hearth-light coming from the drinking hall. Tyrielle was nearly ready to go in and call the baited trap off for the night when she saw a figure, a man she did not know, come into the village from the south with a sour expression on his face. He went immediately into the drinking hall and she heard the sound of shouting voices. Cursing, she moved swiftly to the entrance of the drinking hall to see the regulars scattered and pressed up against the wall, Renias standing in the middle of the room with Arzades in front of him, and the young man with a long blade leveled and gesturing towards Renias with it.

"You lied to me, blacksmith. You're lucky I'm not upset about that. But I'll have the truth from you this time, or I'll stick you through the human shield you've got there," the man demanded, taking a slow, sliding step towards the pair.

Tyrielle watched for a moment, her attention focused on the young man. He looked familiar, but no real bells were ringing in her head as to his identity. But more importantly, he looked like he knew what he was doing. He was a trained swordsman for sure; they could be in trouble. But at the same time, this presented her with an opportunity. She weighed the pros and the cons for a moment, and then uttered a small prayer to Turam under her breath. She caught the attention of Arzades and took off her sword, sheath and all, and tossed it through the air towards him. The act earned the gaze of the young man, a brief flash of recognition of her, before the realization struck in and he turned back to Arzades in time to parry a hastily drawn short sword.

The two began to circle each other, circling that was broken up by the tables and chairs that interfered. Every few steps, Arzades would step in and launch a series of frenzied slashes before he would be forced to retreat, beating away the stranger's sword with a defense that was just as furious. Then the young man attacked, and the difference was clear. The stranger's offense was smooth and fluid, practiced far, far longer than a single day and a half. His sweeping attacks drove Arzades back with every step, until he was against the wall. One more sweep and Arzades ducked the longer blade and thrust out at his opponent. The young man swayed aside and tried to bring his sword down across Arzades' back, but Arzades dropped lower and scampered across the dirt floor, sweeping his hands forward and pulling himself forward as much as he scrambled on the ground with his legs.

A table now between the two of them,

Arzades stood up, one hand clenched at his side, the other flexing around the hilt of the short blade his mother threw to him. He and the as-of-yet unnamed young man stared at each other, Arzades gasping for breath, the young man's chest heaving, but still controlled. Suddenly Arzades launched forward, only to be stymied as his foe kicked the table forward into his thighs, forcing him to retreat, pursued by his foe. Another few blows were exchanged, with no clean hits yet, and Arzades played his last card. He swept his left hand up and across his opponent's face, and released the cloud of dirt he had captured from his earlier scramble across the ground. And unlike his mother, the young man he faced was not nearly as adept at defending himself while blinded. After a few short swipes and bats with the short sword, the longer blade was knocked aside and Arzades levelled his sword across the foe's neck.

    Clearing his eyes after a few moments, the young man looked at Arzades. "You cheated," he complained, pausing to remain very still with the sword at his neck.

    Arzades turned to look at his mother, who had since stepped into the hall. "*Can* I cheat?" he asked, curious, before turning his attention back.

    Tyrielle moved to the young man, holding her hand out and beckoning for the sword. Rueful, the young man complied, and once disarmed, Arzades pulled the blade away, slipping it back into the sheath it was flung to him in. "In a duel? Yes, you can absolutely cheat. In a fight? No such rules apply. And unless I'm mistaken, there were no judges here waiting for us, so, ergo, this was a fight."

Lifting the blade up, she examined it, noting several things at once. It was a proper sword, not decorative. She noticed it had seen thorough use since it had been last cared for. And the family mark above the crossguard was still clear.

"So, you're the Kyrie boy. You weren't even born yet when I left. Why are you looking for me?" she asked, to the puzzlement of Arzades who opened his mouth, but was gestured to silence by his mother, who a moment later beckoned for Arzades to lower his sword as well.

"I was asked to by my father. He wants you to come home. Didn't tell me why," the man said, rolling his neck as the crowd of villagers dispersed to leave the three of them alone, even Renias left to return to his home, having had enough excitement for one day.

"Odd. I barely talked to Lord Kyrie while I was still in the West, let alone since. Curious. But, I have nothing to say to him, and now because we've been found, my son and I will be leaving. Don't try to follow us, boy, or you won't be facing the child next time," she said, taking the sword back from Arzades and buckling it back to her side.

"I have to. I was told not to ret-" the young man started, before he was silenced by the sound of an echoing roar, the flash of light and blast of heat sweeping in through the door of the drinking hall.

Chapter 6

The motley collection of people inside the drinking hall sprinted out into the night, to a scene of fire and destruction. Most of the homes of Arvil were on fire, and a few were in the process of collapsing. The screams of terror and pain were evident to their ears, and the instincts of them all were to begin scouring through the rubble for survivors. But as Tyrielle led the rush to the nearest building, that of Renias' son Marik, Tyrielle suddenly pulled up and stopped, reaching out to grab Renias.

"You don't want to see this, smith," she warned in a hushed tone. When Arzades caught up, followed shortly by the young man that had as of yet only been identified as the "Kyrie boy", he saw the same thing that caught his mother's eye: two pairs of legs sticking out of the rubble of the house. With a twisted cry, Renias rushed forward and, as if possessed, began hauling through the wreckage of the house, ignoring both flame and the crushing weight of stone as he hauled away wreckage with both hands.

The sound of another roaring blast of flame distracted the other three, though, and they turned to look down the thoroughfare of the village. Two figures, one massively muscled and bearing an axe made for combat in one hand, and another slender, of indeterminate gender with no discernable weapon, stood still in the only street of the village. The slender one stood with a delicate hand raised, facing towards another house that stood alight with an eerie colour of white flame. Tyrielle muttered something under her breath and stepped swiftly to the side, grabbing and forcefully pulling Arzades with her.

"Pup, listen carefully, because this is what I've spent so long trying to avoid, so long running away from. These are... for lack of a better term, assassins. They are hunting me, and if they know of your existence, they will definitely continue their hunt for you," she explained in a hushed tone, nearly drowned out over the sound of fire and Renias' frenzied digging for his son and son's wife.

"Then, what do we do, mother? We have to stop them, we have to save the villagers. Or..." he paused, looking to where Renias was and looking distinctly sick.

"I'm going to do something, pup, don't worry about it. It's going to be risky, but no matter what, I want you to stay hidden. You too, Kyrie," she added almost like an afterthought. The young stranger also looked ill.

"They must have followed me here. Let me help, at least," he replied, holding out his hand for the return of his sword.

Tyrielle paused for a few moments before she handed over the sword. She then looked back around the corner to see the two figures just as they demolished another structure.

"Damarion Kyrie! Come out and play with us. I promise you won't be harmed. We just want to know what you found out!" came a soft effeminate shout. Tyrielle's response was to creep around the side of the building and to approach the pair from the darkness behind the houses on the thoroughfare.

"See if you can distract them, boy. But don't get killed. Magefire is a hell of a thing to suffer," she softly called out as she left, an idle left hand tracing the edges of her burns as she crept, sword in hand.

Damarion looked between Renias, who was definitely preoccupied, and Arzades, who looked like nothing so much as a lost farm boy, and took a deep breath, before stepping out into the illumination of the street and walking towards the pair of figures. As he approached, he noticed that only the slender one seemed to be casting fire and destroying the buildings, while the other stood stolid, observant of their surroundings. Every tiny movement of the flames elicited a sudden glance from the larger one. If Tyrielle was going to do something permanent about these two, she would have to be careful *and* Damarion would have to put on a good distraction.

"You know me, but I don't know you. Who are you that's so savage as to destroy an innocent village?" he called out as he approached, long blade still in hand, mouth dry as a desert, his hand flexing on the hilt of the sword.

"Ah, there you are, child. Child of Kenzen Kyrie, who sent you out, curiously, to find the woman that betrayed the Emperor and... what, bring her back? Kill her? Doesn't matter; whatever you say, we know what the truth is," the ungendered one hissed. "You ask our names? My chosen name is Tempest, and this is my brother Iron. We are the Emperor's Chosen, and we have no mandate for you, but we do for the scarred bitch. Tell us everything you know about finding her, and we will remember that our orders don't include you. Otherwise..." the one identified as Tempest trailed off as they raised their hand, and a low, quiet whine filled the air before another blast of what Tyrielle referred to as magefire launched towards another house behind Damarion, illuminating the street with a roaring fire and the thundering sound of an explosion, the debris falling to the sides and the house lurching sideways until it collapsed.

Damarion glanced over his shoulder and

back at the collapsing house before returning his gaze to Tempest. "Please... please just stop this. They've done nothing wrong, nothing against the empire or the Emperor," he pleaded, licking his lips, hoping that Tyrielle would not wait until he was a smoking corpse to act.

"Oh please, cut the sob act. They're Crosslanders, their lives mean nothing to us. They're only as useful as it takes to get you to talk, boy. So... talk, or this keeps happening," Tempest raised their hand again, which elicited a start forward by Damarion. Suddenly, Tempest was obscured by the huge hulk of the man called Iron, axe levelled forward and ready to fight. A quick assessment, and Damarion swore that if he stabbed Iron in the chest, either he would complete the lunge and the blade still wouldn't emerge from the other side, or his blade would snap upon the attempt.

"Now now, Iron. I'm sure he wasn't going to do anything...precipitous. That would only guarantee where he stands in regards to our orders. Please, resume your watch. I'll attend to him within a moment," Tempest remarked from behind Iron, who relented with a solid glare at Damarion before returning to his post at Tempest's back.

"Now, Damarion – is it alright if I use your given name?" Tempest asked, before continuing without an answer, "Where were we? Ah yes. I was threatening to take more meaningless lives, and you were going to tell me what you've found out to stop me," they said, levelling their hand once more. With a grunt of exertion, Damarion lifted his blade and swung it in a narrow arc at Tempest.

Iron intervened. He hauled Tempest out of the way with one hand and knocked aside the blade with his axe in the other and launched a return strike. Three things happened at once, then. Tempest pulled themselves forward to stop Iron's attack; Iron's strike continued, fast, aimed at the neck of Damarion; and Tyrielle launched herself off a nearby roof, blade in hand aimed downwards with her fall.

Chaos ensued. Tempest and Damarion both felt themselves knocked aside by Iron, who, with his axe discarded by one hand, reached out and grabbed Tyrielle's blade with his other hand. There was a spurt of blood and a look of surprise on Tyrielle's face when confronted with Iron's speed, before she was grabbed by the collar of her shirt and Tyrielle was thrown down to the ground beside Damarion.

"So pleased you could join us, Lady Anderwyn. That was quite clever, using the boy as a distraction. Shame you didn't have time to surveil us properly. You'd know that my brother Iron is more than a match for a simple surprise attack," Tempest announced, standing and dusting themselves off before reaching up and caressing Iron's cheek fondly, lifting Iron's axe with some effort and handing it back to their brother. Turning back to Damarion and Tyrielle, they smiled. "The Emperor would like to have words with you, but ordered us to kill you if you put up the slightest hint of a fight. Now, I'm inclined to be generous and still take you with us – you haven't upset Iron yet either, so I don't see any reason why not."

Tyrielle's head was still spinning from being slammed to the ground as she groggily pushed herself up. Looking around, she saw that her blade and Damarion's laid together in union on the other side of Iron and Tempest. Looking to Iron, armed with his axe, and Tempest, whom she had seen conjuring magefire, she took a deep breath, and another, before spitting in Tempest's face. From Tempest's reaction of bland disinterest and resignation, she knew she had sealed her own fate. Looking down to Damarion and back to Tempest, she saw them raise their hand – closing her eyes, she uttered a rapid prayer to the Divine Twins. She heard the slow whine of magefire being conjured, a sound that elicited a maddening itch from her burn scars. But she had not the time to scratch.

But then there were new sounds to meet her ears. She opened her eyes to see Arzades, one arm wrapped around Tempest's throat, the other with a knife to their neck, warding off Iron as a result. Tyrielle scrambled to the swords, sliding Damarion's across the ground to him and lifting her own.

"Mother, I'm sorry, " Arzades called out, prodding Tempest's neck with the knife as he moved around Iron to join his mother, "but I couldn't stand by and do nothing."

Tempest cocked their head as Arzades spoke mouthing, "Mother?" before they looked to Iron and nodded slightly. Before any of the three could react, Iron lifted his hands and a small blast of magefire lashed out and struck Arzades in the arm, forcing him to drop the knife. A second, quicker, blast knocked Arzades backwards, releasing Tempest as a result. Before Tyrielle completed the lunge meant to skewer Tempest, they slid backwards and to the side and slammed a hand to the ground. Cackling hysterically, Tempest looked around as the ground began to swell with a whine and the light of magefire erupted in erratic spurts and sprays.

"Well that is interesting news. Rather than keep playing with you folks, I'm going to have to report that Tyrielle Anderwyn, hero of the rebellion and traitor to the Emperor, has a child. Farewell for now!" They called out as the bubble burst with an explosion of force and fire that knocked Tyrielle, Arzades, and Damarion backwards. By the time the smoke and daze had cleared, Iron and Tempest were nowhere to be seen.

Tyrielle pushed herself up and helped up Arzades, turning to Damarion who got up on his own, and beckoned him towards her. Sheathing her sword, she turned to look for Renias. Going back to Marik's house, the torn and crushed bodies of Marik and his wife presented themselves before the group. Muttering a prayer to Liel, Tyrielle looked around for Renias. Seeing naught, she led them around the ruined crater of the thoroughfare to Renias' forge, to see it victimized by Tempest's magicks too. The sound of sobbing came from the far side of the wreckage, where they found Renias holding an ashen white arm that protruded from the crushing stone of the house.

"Renias... Let's dig her out. You can decide what you want to do then," Tyrielle said softly, reaching out for Renias' shoulder and patting it with as much soothing force as possible. Nodding, swallowing, gulping for air, Renias stood up, and together with Tyrielle and Arzades, set to excavating the body of Alari.

Chapter 7

The surviving villagers came out of their homes and out of the hiding places they had fled to over the course of Iron and Tempest's attack. There was a grim haze to the air, between the smoke and the stench of roasting bodies. Tyrielle helped Renias dig out Alari for a short time before she turned her attention to the villagers, most of whom turned away from her.

"Cursed woman," some would say.

"You brought this on us," others accused. But she offered her help anyways.

"Magefire can't be put out with water. Use dirt, or sand, or anything like that to put it out," she called out, loud enough to be heard by all the village. That piece of information delivered, and her assistance shunned, she returned to the ruined forge. Damarion and Arzades were lifting some of the stones together and heaving them to the side, while Renias took a more careful approach, removing the smaller stones and taking care that no further collapse fell onto Alari's body.

Wordlessly, Tyrielle stood and watched; no space for her to assist in the necessary work. She went into the forge,which had held up better than the house. It took more than a few moments before she was able to find what she was looking for, with all the tools scattered about from the force of the magefire detonations. But she lifted the shovel and walked down to a small flat patch of land between the forge and the dock and began digging. The manual labour felt good after the events of the night. It also afforded her the ability to think, for she and Arzades would have to move, and Arzades now knew exactly who the enemy was that was tracking them down. She had already decided on a move to the north, perhaps she would let Arzades judge for himself a place to settle down, or maybe she would pick one of the cities of the Crosslands to live in. Or the Free Cities as she had considered before, albeit they stood closer to the Western Empire than she was necessarily comfortable with.

Shovel-load of dirt followed shovel-load of dirt, and Tyrielle continued her pondering. There was also the matter of the Kyrie boy, Damarion as Tempest had called him, and what he wanted. She weighed those options while digging for Alari's grave. The most likely answer as for why Kenzen wanted her to come home was to raise rebellion again. The presence of the Emperor's Chosen being here, and so close behind Damarion, meant that the Emperor was more than likely aware already of the possibility of rebellion. The only question now was, how aware of the resources available to the rebellion was he. If the limits of his knowledge was just the Kyries, then it might be a while before he acted – the Kyries were one of the original noble families of the West, by legend and lore they even predated the Divine Emperor himself. They would not be a favourable target to remove out of hand.

But at the same time, she thought, Arzades was of an age that he could be left alone to take care of himself. He was already well on his way to becoming a practiced swordsman, and his capturing of Tempest left no doubts as to his capability to make hard decisions sometimes. She would have to inspect his wounds, though. Magefire was a tenacious beast, and if it was not extinguished, it would just continue consuming. At the same time, she remembered words from Myr about the stuff. "Magefire doesn't like to consume mages. It's our ally, not our bane. Our living tool, not just a flame," he half rhymed, as he was wont to do. Tyrielle smiled in remembrance and laid the shovel briefly to rest. Hopping out of the as-of-yet still shallow hole, she went back into the ruins and stepped to Arzades. As he and Damarion laid the next rock aside, Tyrielle took his arm gently and lifted it, checking the scorch-marked hole in his shirt. It did not seem like the wound was worsening, and as she moved her eyes to the blast-mark in his shoulder, it also did not seem too bad. In fact, it seemed to be partially healed already, a fact that caught her by surprise.

"What is it?" Arzades asked, looking between his mother and the mark on his shoulder. "Nothing, pup. Nothing serious. I was just making sure that the flames had gone out. Magefire is nothing to take lightly, and I know that better than most. I wanted to make sure you were going to be okay, and it looks like you'll be fine. Now get back to work; I'll get back to digging a grave for Alari," earning a half-sob from Renias behind her.

***

A few hours later, into the early morning by this point, they laid Alari, wrapped in a quilt that she had made for herself and Renias during the days she was pregnant with their first child Marik, into the deep grave Tyrielle dug.

"It seemed the best thing we could wrap her in," Damarion said, to which Renias half nodded in appreciation, tears still streaking down his face from moment to moment. The quartet was joined by Eillel, Renias' daughter who had survived the attack, who was weeping in mourning for her mother. As Tyrielle watched, Renias grabbed a handful of dirt and tossed it into the grave onto the body.

With a shaky voice he recited, "May Liel take

you into her grace. May Liel guide you home and let you rest. May Turam be the guardian at the gates of your resting place, and may Liel sing you songs of salvation and tranquility," and stepped back. Tyrielle, with help from Damarion and Arzades, pushed the dirt into the hole over the course of minutes until all that was left was the mound, which Tyrielle took care in gently packing down.

Eillel embraced her father tightly, the tears falling down both their faces, "She'll rest well, papa. You did what you could."

"I could have been here with her, at least," he replied, wiping his face clear.

"What would that have solved? Then I'd be burying two parents," she chastised, reaching up and caressing her father's cheek. He flinched away briefly, then nodded, taking a deep, shuddering breath.

"Go on, get you back home, Eillel. You've got more than just yourself to care for, now, and your mother isn't going to be able to help you now. Start talking to the other women with children in the village, if any are left," he ended bitterly, still staring at the gravesite.

Nodding, Eillel dipped her head towards Tyrielle and her son, before backing away and returning to the headman's house. Tyrielle beckoned to Damarion and Arzades and together they walked back up into the house to give Renias some degree of privacy.

Pulling aside the sole surviving chair, Tyrielle sat down, clasping her hands together and looking up at the two young men. She was forced to realize that Arzades was in fact a young man, and that he and Damarion were of similar age to each other.

"We have a problem, Kyrie, pup. So I'm going to tell you why we have a problem, and then we can decide what we're doing going forward from this. Arzades... I haven't told you this before, but I fled in secret while I was pregnant with you, before I was showing signs. So no-one back home knows you exist, and that was the way I wanted it. If they knew there was an heir to your father's rebellion, we'd have never known peace or tranquility. Tempest making it back home to make a report on your existence is a large problem we now have to deal with."

"So, boys, what do we do next?" she asked. The two of them looked to each other.

"If Iron and Tempest return home to make their report, then we'll never be safe. I'll be looking over my shoulder every day, even if we run as far as the eastern edges of the Salt Waste. I want to go after them," Arzades stated

Damarion spoke up in addition, "We may very well have to kill them. Servants of the Emperor are no laughing matter. A simple negotiation, whether threat or bribe, won't turn them. So death it might have to be."

Tyrielle blinked in slow thought at that

notion. "They've got a head start on us now, and we don't know where they went for sure. Trying to track them is a ludicrous notion," she replied.

"That's the thing. I don't think it is. If they tracked me here, then they followed in my footsteps. I believe all we have to do is retrace my steps to travel here, and we'll find their trail in no time," Damarion said, brushing a thumb across his lips in a kind of nervous excitement.

"What's your horse in this race, Kyrie?" she responded, curious as to the cooperation between the two men now.

"Well, I still have my father's orders, there is that. By helping in doing this, I was hoping that, in addition to getting vengeance for these helpless villagers, I would be able to convince you to join me after all. I suspect now that I know exactly who you are, I know why my father wants you to come back. And I can't say I disagree. Things are getting worse in the West. The nobles are given a free hand to act as tyrants over their subjects, and one of the last realms that chaos hasn't infested as a result is the Kyrie lands. The Emperor continues to permit and encourage the behaviours for his own amusement. Father's been in contact with some people who're trying to raise rebellion, but it's slow. So slow. And because it's slow, it's alive, but at the same time, there's no fire, no fervent belief in the cause," he stated, pacing about the now-small room as he spoke, "The only other holdout was the Anderwyn family lands, but the Emperor ended that family seventeen years ago, or so we were told. If you were to appear and join us, even better both of you, it would launch the rebellion into full sway."

Tyrielle held up a hand to stop Damarion's spiel and thoughtfully half-pursed her lips. Her right hand reached up to trace the scars along the side of her face. He was right, after a fashion, and on top of that, where she had an army of captains willing to side with her and her cause when she turned coat, now those same captains would be generals and commanders.

"Alright boys, I've decided. The first thing we'll do is track down those two mages and stop them from making their report. After that, we'll decide on the next step. But I'm inclined to follow you home, Kyrie. It's time to try and do something about the chicanery and crudity of the Western Empire now. Arzades... I don't want you coming with us, though."

"What? Why not? Clearly I'm capable enough to be of use," he stammered briefly, before Tyrielle's upheld palm stopped him.

"It's not because you're capable or not, pup. I've got a much more important job for you. You're going to learn how to be a mage proper," she ordered, to the surprise of Damarion and Arzades both. "Once we've caught up with those two mages, I want you to travel to Ketheria itself, and seek out a mage there for a teacher. And once you have learned your magicks, then I want you to come join us in the West. No rebellion can possibly succeed in the West without the aid of a mage, and a powerful one at that. You'll be powerful enough – your father saw to that – but you need the training to be able to use any of it."

"I... see," Arzades replied, mulling over the thought. Obviously he did not care to be separated from his mother, but at the same time, the notion of becoming a mage and being able to be a real force for change in the West? Now that was something that caught the attention of the wonder-seeker in him.

Damarion nodded in agreement, "No doubt another sword would always be useful, but our enemies have countless mages on their behalf, flinging wild magefire and assorted other disasters at will. If you've got the chance to become a mage? Take it and then be even more useful to us," he added on to Tyrielle's considerations.

Arzades nodded slowly, before he responded, "Alright. Then that's what I'll do. But first comes catching Iron and Tempest."

Tyrielle nodded and stood up. Seeing Renias behind the two men, she called out, "Blacksmith, I'm sorry, so sorry, for you and your's loss. We'll do our best to avenge them on the bodies of the mages who did this."

"No you won't," Renias responded in a croaking voice, and moving into the kitchen, he dug around in a great chest attached to the wall, eventually pulling a war axe free of the chest, "I'm coming with you," he said, flexing his hand on the haft of the axe and giving it a few test swings.

"So, I was right. You were a soldier, weren't you," she stated, nodding in reply to his coming along.

"Was a soldier. Was a blacksmith. Now I'm just going to be a killer," he said, slamming the axe blade into the wooden part of the wall, carving a large swath of wood from the wall, before he dug a sling for the axe out of the chest as well, and strapping it on, stepped between the other three. "Day's wasting, come on," he said, leaving his forge for the last time.

Chapter 8 - First Interlude

The two of them looked so very much alike. They were twins, of course. But more than that, they were born in the same moment, neither older or younger than the other. For the now, they sat in silence, content to let the sounds of the tavern they occupied wash over them. They sat, him with his back to the wall, guarded and secure and on watch for trouble. They sat, her with her back open to the entire tavern. She was dressed in a white gown, as purely white as fresh fallen snow, seemingly unstainable by the atmosphere of the tavern. He was dressed in a motley selection of armours, boiled leather, chain in some places, plates of metal in others. He was also armed with an assortment of weapons – several small throwing knives, a short sword of some variety on his right hip, a longer sword of some weight on his left hip. The table sat empty between them. Neither of them were inclined to drink, least of all anything the tavern was inclined to serve them.

Minutes passed with silence being the only thing passed between the two siblings, before he spoke, "How do you think they'll do this time?" as he shifted to recline back in the chair.

She rested a nearly-ivory coloured hand on the table before she replied, "They've got a chance. Not much more than that. All the pieces that they have are currently in play now. All that's left is intermediary business and then the face off at the end. Then we'll see where things stand."

He nodded and responded, "And I take it you want to remain out of it. You know we could involve ourselves and it wouldn't risk anything. In fact, we'd probably be more successful than they ever will be."

"True. But I don't want to set a precedent where they will come to find themselves at our doorstep, so to speak, every time something goes wrong. I care for them much, but I want to see them grow past the need for us."

"I find that reasonable. But at the same time, I ache to find something to do, dear sister. Something worthy of us."

Finally she smiled a beneficent smile, one that, if they had noticed the table at all, would have drawn the attention of every person in the tavern within seconds. But no-one seemed to see the table, even when they looked directly at it.

"Brother, if there is an issue that is truly worthy of our attention, then they will have long since failed and we'll be in such a kettle of trouble, the likes of which we haven't seen since..." she trailed off as he raised his hand and looked around.

"No protection is perfect, and things like that are better off not spoken of at all. Not when you can communicate just well enough without it," he warned, to which she nodded and looked around herself. It seemed like none had overheard them talking, but there was no guarantee with these people, not with how clever and deceiving they continuously proved themselves.

"You're right of course, dear brother. It seems like nothing's been done that we need to do anything about here. But perhaps we'd better not press our luck any further. I'll see you next holiday," she said, smiling beatifically, before she stood and started making her way out of the tavern. As she stepped away from the table, she seemed to draw the attention of everyone in the tavern. Her brother stood up, already ready to make a move upon the first person that deigned to touch her. The room fell silent as she picked her way between the tables until she had almost made it to the door, when one drunkard reached out to grab at her. He found his hand clutching at air, when her brother reached out and grabbed him by the shoulder, hauling him up.

His sister could not see what the people of

the tavern saw, but she could imagine it, knowing her brother's inclinations. The patrons of the tavern saw a sudden deepening of the shadows, a chill growing in the air until each and every one of them could see their breaths hanging in clouds. The perpetrator winced in agony as her brother's grip tightened on his shoulder, a dark glare in his eyes as he forced the man to meet his eyes. What he saw there, no other man saw, but he became as white as a sheet. After a few moments passed, her brother released the man from his grip and the atmosphere of the tavern returned to normal. As the man rubbed his shoulder, he looked up to see who had done this, to see the woman that had so fired his emotions again, to find them both departed, him dressed in dark colours and blacks, she in purest white.

At the next intersection they turned to part ways, him turning into a deep, dark alleyway, her turning into a grand wide square, well lit, filled with kiosks and carts of merchants closed up for the night, and a grand fountain with five great statues of the same person in different poses of athletic perfection at the four corners and the centre. Taking a seat at the edge of the fountain and the foot of one of the statues, she reached into the basin and lifted a handful of water, just to watch it drip back into the fountain basin. As the droplets fell into the basin, she began to sing in a language long since forgotten by people.

All things that come to pass

And all things that come to rest
All shall be silent
All shall be still
All that will, will come to roost
And all that will, will stay away
And all that will, will stand themselves still
All will rest
All will lay still

The new day will dawn
And all will come forth
All that were still
Will no longer be forced
The green light will grow
And fuel the earth's growth
And all that rested
And all that were still
Will see a new day before them

People paused as she sang. They did not know the words, but she sang her song so beautifully that to them, it did not matter that they did not know. They were awestruck by her voice and her beauty alone. Several people tried to approach, but at the last second, turned shy and turned away. At last, when she finished her song, there was the sound of a single applauder before even that fell silent. And she picked her way through the crowd once more and wandered down the streets of the city, humming softly a tune that no one knew.

Chapter 9

Renias led the group as they picked their way along the outskirts of the village. Tyrielle still earned a few scowls from the ones who observed, a few spat in her direction even, but they were distant enough that the animosity wore down before it became a problem. Once past the last of the houses, they turned north and began following the 'road', such as it was. It was mostly a beaten footpath alongside the forest. "I want to march at least until midday before we take a break – we have no idea the speed at which our enemies are traveling, and we neither want to come upon them unaware, nor do we want to fall behind them too far," Renias commented as they started on their journey northwards.

"Yes, right. To that end, I came here from

Citadel Kyrie, passed through the Free Cities, and then Mereketh, Isolis, and Elard, before I turned southwards and found a village where they directed me here. I think our first stop should be that village, to make sure we're following on the right trail," Damarion stated, looking between the others and seeing nods of affirmation.

As they continued north, Tyrielle suddenly started, looking around. "There's something I have to go do. Keep travelling, I'll catch up soon enough," she said, taking off at a loping half-run, disappearing into the grove of trees connected to the forest nearby. Arzades lifted his hand in a half-effort to call her back, but let it fall to his side again. Nervous now, Arzades turned back to the others and jogged for a quick second to catch up, falling in step beside Damarion and behind Renias.

***

Under the midday sun, Renias let the two younger men rest, while he began foraging for foodstuffs in the nearby woods. Arzades looked to Damarion, taking a measure of this young man that just suddenly became a part of their lives. Dark, chestnut brown hair, medium length. About the same height as Arzades, a little smaller but also more fit. Green eyes, like emeralds. His mother always said that green eyes were a sign of the Emeraldsea, so the comparison felt apt.

"Was it your mother who taught you to fight?" Damarion asked suddenly, drawing Arzades' attention.

"Yes, it was. What does it matter?"

"Nothing much. I had some of the finest duelling instructors that could be found, and you still managed to take me down. Using a cheap trick, but you still did it," he replied, taking a rough cloth and a stone from his pack and sitting down to care for his sword.

"Ah. Then, you wouldn't be pleased, I suppose, to learn that I've only been practicing for two days now?" Arzades returned, smirking, an edge of irritation with this nobleman.

Damarion paused in the tending to his sword, starting to chuckle which evolved into a full-hearted belly laugh. "You mean I got beaten by a country bumpkin who wasn't fully trained and still barely had to resort to trickery to beat me?" he howled with laughter, earning a chuckle in turn from Arzades.

"Basically, yes, city boy," he drawled, playing up the countryside accent the other villagers of Arvil came by honestly, earning another howl of laughter from Damarion.

"I'm glad you haven't been practicing much longer than that, then. Who knows what would have happened in that drinking hall, then?"

"There was enough of us there, I don't think you'd have been forward enough to do anything drastic, not while surrounded. And Arzades, for his part, would have hesitated before striking anything like a final blow," came the voice of Renias as he came back from his foraging efforts, bundles of root vegetables and berries in his hands. "Come here, boys. I'm going to show you what to look for on the road for scavenging for food," he added, laying down his catch to begin teaching foraging to the two young men. Arzades already knew most of the knowledge Renias tried to pass along, so his attention wandered, wondering where his mother had gone, only to be called back to the immediate area whenever Damarion asked a question.

"Oh, did we find food already? Excellent, I'm starving after that bit of work," called out a familiar female voice. Tyrielle came up to the trio from the south, a burlap bundle on her back. As she approached, she slung it off her back and tossed it to Arzades. The hilt of a gorgeous longer sword, straight edged, stuck out of the folds. The blade itself looked like it required some work before it would be serviceable again, but the hilt shone with gold inlays and gemstones, mostly blue with red stones for accents. Wrapping his hand around the hilt, he pulled the sword free of the burlap, and the blade caught the sun's light easily. Even with the necessary attendance to it, it was still clear that the blade was high quality steel. Experimenting with a few swings, Arzades noted the weight of the blade was significantly different from his mother's shorter blade. He looked to her, noting the shovel marked with fresh dirt on it, the dirt-marked sack at her side, and the dirty stains on the burlap.

"Where did this come from, mother?" he asked, curious to know, but imagining he already knew the answer.

"Your father's memorial stone was more than that, it also marked where I buried the sword he gave me when we got married. I never liked how gaudy he had it made, but he'd always crack the same jokes whenever I complained about it. So I buried it and got Renias to make me a simple beater of a short sword."

Arzades nodded at that, turning the sword over and examining it from all sides, before rewrapping it into the burlap sack and offering it back to his mother.

"No no, pup. That's yours now. Your sword and your problem," she said, refusing the bundle. Nodding, he lifted the bundle carefully, judging its weight before slinging it onto his back. The time passed in silence as they consumed their scant foraged goods, Renias looking at the bundle once before nodding to Tyrielle wordlessly.

"Next time we take a break, I'll show you how I care for my sword, bumpkin. And then maybe we'll be able to negotiate tools from the next village so you can care for your own," Damarion said, standing up and dusting himself off.

"After we get it properly fixed up, I see no reason why not," said Renias, voice no longer creaking with the effects of grief.

Arzades chose that inopportune moment to yawn. "Something the matter, pup?" Tyrielle called over as they got ready to head up and leave.

"Just that we're rolling into the second day

being straight-awake, mother. Not something I'm used to," Arzades replied, stretching his neck from side to side before nodding to Renias, who started following the road north again. Damarion fell in beside him and Tyrielle held up the rear.

"Just be thankful we're not on the high seas. I remember one time I was out there on a fishing trip as an apprentice, that we got caught in a storm. All hands were awake for close to three days straight as the storm carried us along before finally letting us go. And then I was one of the unlucky ones that went on watch after that, just to rub it in. I think the captain just had it in for me, the nobleman's son who was out there on a lark. Never mind the fact that father had to order me onto the boat in the first place, clearly that wasn't enough evidence I didn't want to be there either. But after that watch, you couldn't wake me by dunking me in the ocean, I was that tired. Never felt a bed so comfortable as my hammock that afternoon, either." Damarion regaled the others with the tale as they walked along.

Arzades looked over at him and looked him up and down, before returning his gaze to the path ahead. "I'm surprised you decided against that life for a career. Sounds like it would be a real blast of excitement," he commented, slashing the air with an imaginary sword.

"You'd think so, but we were at sea for ten days instead of the week we were supposed to be. And that regular week, by the Empty Heaven itself was it ever boring. Cast out nets, reel in nets. Cast out nets, reel in nets. Salt the fish, try not to vomit from the overwhelming fish smell, then cast more nets again. The most exciting thing that happened was a dolphin sighting – other than that, we had calm seas and clear air the entire fishing trip. I'm sure that's what every captain dreams of, but to a boy that was dreaming of the exciting life on the seas, beyond that three day storm? It was a terrible disappointment," Damarion replied, earning a chuckle from both Arzades and Tyrielle. Renias remained silent.

"What's a dolphin?" Arzades asked, tilting his head, "I'm guessing some kind of fish?"

"More a good luck sign than a fish, sailors say. But it looked beautiful, so I, and the others on the ship, left it alone. The sailors' chatter went on for hours about how they'd been blessed," Damarion explained, waving his hands in the air to indicate size as he spoke.

Arzades smiled, slightly in awe of the nobleman's tale. "Just about the most exciting thing that happened to me was one time I was on my regular hike - there's a spot I like to call Phoenix Rock, right? - and I loved to climb this rock. It was a massive ten metre cliff face, with numerous places you can stop and sit along the way. I liked to sit at the second highest point and just look over the forest. I called it my 'Emeraldsea', since it looked like what I imagined the open sea to look like. Anyways, I was up there once when a hawk dived at me, a great old bastard of a bird, and nearly knocked me off the Rock. I slid off the top seat and fell from handhold to handhold all the way down to the next seat, where I finally caught myself," Arzades replied, which earned him a reaction from Damarion, who had paled slightly and shook his head.

"Not for me, rock climbing. I couldn't do the crow's nest either. But I got really good about the work on the deck itself, just so they couldn't make me go up there," he replied, looking back to Tyrielle who had levelled a solid, steady glare into the back of Arzades' head. Looking between the two of them quickly, Damarion stepped to the side to clear himself from the incoming disaster zone.

"You never told me about that," Tyrielle bit off like every word was a solid thing. Arzades cringed as he heard her speak.

"I didn't think it was such a big deal, mother. After all, I survived, didn't I?" he quipped, turning to look at her.

Turning into a full arm slap that nearly knocked him from his feet. "I don't normally hold with hitting children, but you're an adult now..." she started to say, when Arzades interrupted.

"I'm an adult now? When did that happen? I was told there'd be cake," he quipped again, earning himself another full-bodied slap that caused his ears to ring and eyes to shimmer with sparkling lights.

"Boy, you just don't know when to quit, do

you?" she said, brushing errant silver hairs out of her face as she stared at her son, "You know I worried about you when you started climbing that rock. You being so good at it and safe is the only reason I continued to let you, and then you come out with this? I am not impressed, pup," she said, the hints of anger beginning to fade in favour of worried concern.

Arzades stood up straight and, taking a moment to straighten his clothing before he looked back to meet his mother's gaze, looking slightly away from meeting her eyes. A moment passed, and then another, before he spoke again, "I thought you always said to never quit; I was just doing what you said."

Tyrielle stomped her foot angrily and exhaled a held breath before kicking her son solidly in the shin, causing him to jump and limp around as she passed him to catch up to Renias.

As she passed, Damarion looked over to Arzades and remarked, "For what it's worth, I thought it was funny," which he followed with a massive exhalation of air as Tyrielle kicked him square in the stomach, causing him to collapse, coughing for a few moments while Arzades limped over and helped him back up.

"Maybe we shouldn't say anything for a bit," Arzades suggested, earning a nod from Damarion as they fell in step behind their two elders.

What they did not see was the slight half smirk on her face.

Chapter 10

They came upon the nearest village the next day around mid-afternoon. Tyrielle led them to the village headman's house and knocked on the door briskly. A few moments passed before a large man in a well-off coat – for the kind of village they were in – answered the door.

"Yes, might I help you?" he asked, in a kind of raspy voice.

"Yes, we're trying to catch up to some friends of ours. One is a fairly small person, not much to them at all, but the other is a big old bastard of a man. We're just wondering if they passed through the village at all?" Tyrielle asked, the others relaxing nearby.

"Oh, those two. Yeah, they came through a few days ago asking after someone, and then just yesterday I believe, they came back the other way, but didn't stop to ask anyone anything that time around." he replied, reaching up and scratching his head, "To be honest, I didn't care much for them. They seemed too focused and not quite all there, and you can't trust people like that around."

Tyrielle laughed softly and nodded. "Yes, they've been like that as long as I've known them. Anyways, thank you so very much for the help – we'd better be off if we're looking to catch up to them before they hit Elard," she replied, beckoning to the others and heading off to the side of the house.

"Do you think they have enough tents, bedrolls and the like here to serve our needs?" she asked, mostly of Renias.

"Likely not. They might have the materials on hand to make them, but it's unlikely they have them already ready for us. And I don't want to wait," he grumbled, getting nods from the others.

"Let's at least get some rudimentary supplies and what we can for the travel northwards," she replied, taking them to the lone building with open sides to it, a building that served as a kind of general store. Perusing the store for a few minutes, she directed Arzades and Damarion to grab a few things; some packs of jerky and other preserved goods, and a solitary bedroll and tent. Reaching into the sack Tyrielle procured at the same time as Arzades' sword, she produced a pair of silver coins and offered them to a mostly awestruck shopkeeper. Shopping completed, and items distributed fairly amongst the four of them, Renias led them towards the village's main gate – their only gate – and they broke free from the edge of the village, realigning themselves to travelling north.

"What I wouldn't give to have some proper horses right now," Tyrielle grumbled.

Renias nodded at that. "Would make it a lot easier to control when we catch up to the bastards, for sure," he said, flexing his right hand and half-heartedly reaching for the war axe on his back.

"Now now, now isn't yet the time for that, Renias. But soon," she cautioned, placing a hand on the smith's shoulder, as they continued northward.

***

They met up with the Southern Highway shortly before nightfall that day. They travelled onwards for about another hour before Tyrielle motioned to a nearby grove of trees, where they took shelter and set up their meager accommodations. The tent was large enough for two people, so they planned out a shift rotation so that one would always be awake, allowing for the tent and the bedroll to always be used.

They ate from their humble supply of jerky and other items. Before turning in, Arzades turned to Damarion and asked "Would you care to indulge me in another match, Sir Kyrie?" Damarion smirked for a moment and nodded. Taking his mother's sword again, Arzades drew it from its sheath and turned to face Damarion. A moment's pause, and the two of them were off, striking at each other and blocking or otherwise evading each other's strikes. Tyrielle watched the two of them carefully, calling out advice and warnings in equal measure as the contest got heated to the point of overwhelming excitement. Content that even now the two of them would not hurt each other badly, Tyrielle returned her attention to the small, concealed campfire that served as their light and warmth.

"Never thought I'd be going home. Let alone with my son in tow," she said, mostly to nobody but earning a nod from Renias anyways.

"I never thought a lot of things. I didn't expect to ever pick this up again," he said, patting the war axe beside him for emphasis, "I didn't expect to leave that village for anything more than supplies for my forge. Didn't expect to outlive my son," he said, pausing, choked up for a moment, "Didn't expect to bury my wife so soon, or that I'd need the villagers to bury my son for me,"

Tyrielle nodded with each proclamation Renias uttered. "For what it's worth, Renias, I'm so sorry. I didn't expect the agents of the Emperor to be so indiscriminate. Nor did I expect them to find me at all. I'm sorry that it's my presence that led to this, so sorry that it took so much of your family from you," she whispered softly, the words barely carrying themselves across the fire and over the sounds of the two young men fighting in the background.

"I don't blame you, Tyrielle. You were just protecting what you held dear. I blame the ones that actually took my life from me, not the reason they were here," he replied, his grumbling growing louder, angrier as it went on.

"Still. You have my deepest sympathies and apologies, for what they're worth. And when we catch up to them, they're yours to decide what to do with," she stated emphatically, getting a nod from Renias.

"Thank you, for that. For everything you've done and are trying to do. I don't expect my mind to change much between then and now."

Tyrielle nodded in turn. "I expected as much, and can't say I bear them much sympathy. Only thing I know of to buy them leniency or put them in their graves for sure is this; in order to become the Emperor's Chosen, you have to be some of the most vicious, cunning, and powerful people."

Renias laughed harshly, running a hand over his face."You say that to buy them leniency? I'd better make sure not to fall on your bad side, then," he responded.

Tyrielle smirked, flicking a small stick into the fire. "And then you endure a month long training from the Divine Emperor himself. As of the time I left the West, only two survived that training and were still considered sane," she continued, earning a look from Renias that was a confluence of emotions. "And they were used like tools, swords that were beaten into plowshares, plowshares that were beaten into wreckage. They didn't survive long. I think the Emperor genuinely fears his Chosen, and so tries to drive them insane or break them otherwise."

"What a horrid thing to do to people. But to me, it sounds like they are rabid dogs, only good for being put down," the blacksmith replied coldly, a tone which Tyrielle could only match by nodding in agreement. The two of them watched the fire flicker for a few moments in mostly silence, the clashing of swords in the background the only discernible sound.

"So, Iron and Tempest... what are their insanities, their weaknesses?" Renias asked, after the moments had passed, biting into a piece of jerky and chewing it thoughtfully.

"In the short time I was observing, I noticed this – Tempest never moved without Iron being constantly at their back, unless Iron was actively engaged with fighting someone, in which it became instantly the other way around. I think they are entirely too codependent. If we can separate them somehow, I think that will be the key to defeating them."

"What of their individual strengths and weaknesses?"

"Tempest is obviously nothing much physically, but if I had to guess, he's among the strongest mages of this age. And Iron, while he is still a mage as we saw, seems to have forsaken that all in favour of the physical. I've never seen a man as large as him," Tyrielle admitted, poking the fire with a stick, idly stirring up the coals.

"So basically we have some of the strongest in their fields, driven mad by the Emperor's teaching. And we're hunting them down," Renias muttered, shaking his head, "I don't have any choice now, but if you lot cared to jump ship, I wouldn't blame you."

"No, Renias, we've all got our reasons to want to bring them down. Yours are just more personal than ours. But that doesn't mean our motivations don't exist."

Renias nodded at that, and for a while the camp was silent except for the sounds of exchanged sword blows and exertion made by the young men. Tyrielle turned her gaze to watching the two of them hack and slash at each other. At this point they were full into the swing of things, and any advice she would call out would be unheeded at best, dangerously distracting at worst. So she contented herself with observing.

The two of them were a study in even-matchedness. For all that Arzades had only been practicing a couple of days, he was an exceptionally fast learner and had been studying his mother all these years while she practiced.

Damarion had more training, and formally at that, but it was obvious he had very little tempering in actual fights, not duels, and Arzades was taking full advantage of that. Every time Damarion made an advance on Arzades that he could not block or evade, he would use the trees for cover and come around striking from the other side. This would force Damarion back a few steps, until he recovered and launched his own offensive. Rinse and repeat infinitely, or until one of them tired.

A few minutes of watching, and Tyrielle decided it was enough, that it was time for rest. Lifting her fingers to her lips, she blew a hard, sharp whistle that cut through the silent night and the sound of the fight to reach the two of them. Breathing hard, they both returned to the campfire, Arzades sitting on the bedroll and Damarion taking a seat on a fallen log nearby.

"That's good enough for tonight, boys. Tomorrow, if we haven't reached Elard, we'll do this again. I'll tell you everything you did wrong the night before, and we'll continue like this until we're no longer traveling together," she said, earning a scoff from Damarion which in turn earned a look from both Arzades and Tyrielle, "You were hacking and slashing away for almost ten minutes straight, Kyrie, and neither of you managed to touch the other. I call that close."

Damarion was forced to nod at that, still breathing heavily from the exertion. "Training to fight other swordsmen doesn't do you a whole lot of good when you're not fighting someone who doesn't have formal training, I've noticed," he stated, starting to take deliberately deep breaths to calm his breathing.

"And I've noticed that I can't break his guard, not without a trick of some kind," Arzades admitted, earning himself a nod.

"That will come in time. You'll start to see the dozen small flaws in any person's defense, given enough time. You just have to fight them long enough to get them to show their weaknesses to you," Tyrielle taught, "You can get by without skill and without luck, if you just have more endurance than the other fighter. The first two help, and it will be hard to win without those, but with endurance, your opponent will eventually become sloppier, more desperate, make bigger mistakes, and all you have to do at that point is capitalize on them."

Arzades nodded again, followed by Damarion, and when they replied, Tyrielle continued, "That's the crux of how I became the dueling champion of the West. I wore down my opponents, bided my time, gave them no openings while I waited for one to present itself. As I mentioned before, Arzades, it's the 'economy of effort'. The less energy you spend early on, the more you'll have for the fight later. Or, in some cases, the next fight, or the fight after that."

Arzades laid down and stretched out on the bedroll. "I'll keep that in mind, mother. I'll have to get you to show me how to remain so still as you do, someday. But for now, I'm just tired enough to sleep. It's been a really long few days," he replied, yawning and closing his eyes to doze.

Tyrielle looked to Damarion, who had since composed himself and stood there, looking around into the darkness of the night. "You're up for taking first watch, Kyrie?" Damarion nodded in reply and both Renias and Tyrielle stood up. Tyrielle stretching first with Renias hobbling into the tent, holding the flap aside for Tyrielle as well.

Once inside the tent, Renias fell asleep nearly instantly, while Tyrielle stared at the tent ceiling for a few moments yet. Strategy after strategy whirling through her head about Iron and Tempest and the three men she had at her side.

Chapter 11

The stars whirled above them as each of them slept and as each of them took their turn on watch. But Tyrielle's sleep did not go undisturbed. Instead, she dreamed of a night from seventeen years ago that turned into the longest night of her life. She remembered the night of fire and blood and loss.

It started off simply enough. Portions of the Imperial Army that were loyal to her had begun pouring into the Anderwyn winter retreat. Their numbers, combined with the retainers of the nobles that were loyal to the rebel cause, could make them a serious contender for control over the country. But they had to organize first, and that took time. So much time. Tyrielle remembered them finally being ready to make a strike against the Imperial loyalists, only to receive news that the core of the Imperial Army was on its way to meet them already. Then came the night of fire.

Army against army, facing off along the green valley where normally there was no traffic until the snow was well on the ground. But even so, out of season as it was, the land was a beautiful place. And, as many thought, it would be a beautiful place to die. Tyrielle stood on the parapets of the winter retreat's keep, and looked across the valley. They were outnumbered, as some forces had yet to rally to the rebel cause, but Tyrielle knew the generals, at least as well as they knew themselves, and she was trained directly by the foremost strategist of the age, her father. She was confident that, barring any foreign elements, her forces would walk away from this encounter with a victory in their tally column.

The only unknown belonged to the ivory and scarlet banner that stood at the core of the enemy forces. She had never seen it before, nor had her father, but stories had been passed down of a time when that banner was seen everywhere – the banner of the Divine Emperor himself. Said to be the strongest mage of an age long past, a man long past his years to be alive; none living or dead had seen him unleash his full powers anywhere. With him, he usually had a few of the Emperor's Chosen; bodyguards and agents that he used as his hands and eyes and dirty workers. But this time it looked like he stood alone.

Compared to this, they had Myr Anderwyn, widely regarded as the greatest practicing mage of the time, as adept at wielding magefire as he was the finer elements of magery. Given time, she felt that Myr would be prepared for everything the Emperor could throw at them... but that was the thing. Did they have the time? Tyrielle breathed in deeply and looked out upon the field of battle. Lifting her hand in signal, a small group of mounted horsemen rode forth, bearing a banner of truce and waited in the mid point between the two armies. Long, long moments passed before a similar contingent exited the loyalist forces. The conference took approximately five minutes before both sides retreated to their respective battle lines, and Tyrielle waited for their negotiator's report.

"They've offered terms of surrender, offered that if you and your husband turn yourselves in to Imperial custody, the other nobles will be allowed to return to their lands after swearing their oaths of loyalty to the Emperor himself. The military forces that joined you will face decimation, commanders and leaders not being exempt, but that will be the limit of their punishment," the negotiator reported when he finally joined Tyrielle.

"How generous. I know what Myr's answer would be. How about the other nobles, and the commanders of the army?"

"Mixed answers. Mostly against the surrender – the army remains loyal to you, of course. And the nobles for the most part are loyal to Myr and the cause."

"Excellent. Make a note of the ones who were unsure and the ones openly for the trade. We'll discuss things with the latter, after this particular battle is ended," she ordered, not knowing that it would not be relevant in the slightest, that this battle was fated to be lost.

The negotiator nodded and returned to the courtyard where the rest of the negotiating team awaited. They headed out once more to the meeting point where they would announce the refusal of the terms and hostilities would officially begin. Tyrielle sighed and shook her head dismissively at the waste of life that was soon to occur.

"Regrets, love?" came the voice of Myr and the warmth of his embrace soon wrapped around her.

"Of course, sweets. We're about to be killing our own people. And for what? A minor disagreement over the way that things should be done."

"Not minor, my love. The Divine Emperor has given the nobles too free a hand to deal with their respective realms. Some are taking that as license to indulge their darkest whims. And he won't rein them in. So we have to do something about it. We are doing something about it. Something that only we could have done together. We don't have the numbers of the nobles on our side – they've been bought by their own licentious appetites. But we do have far more of the army than I was expecting on our side."

"I know that, sweets. But, it looks like we're out of time. The negotiators are on their way back, and I suspect that as soon as they're both within their lines, things will start to move. Are the archers ready?" she called out, receiving an affirmative answer. They had already tested out the max range of the archers, and they would be peppering the loyalist forces with arrows for a minute if they marched, less so if they charged. It would not have a lot of effect, but anything they could do to tilt the balance of war would reduce the loss of life on their side at least.

The expected probing charge came, and Tyrielle was suddenly busy with messenger after messenger, sending out orders and receiving reports in kind. Myr backed away, off to make more of his own preparations. The outer walls were being loaded up with wards against magefire, wards that were a particular specialty of Myr's. He did not know if they would hold up with what the Emperor could release upon them, but until the Emperor was on the field, this was all he could do.

Tyrielle itched to be down there in the fight herself, but she knew she would be a liability. No stranger to duels or to rules-free fights, she did not have the same kind of stamina that it took to be a soldier. To wear that kind of armor and carry that shield – she could, she had done it when putting down rebellions in the past, but that was not where her expertise was.

As the commander, she needed to be findable at all times of the battle. Her musing became interrupted as she issued orders for the vanguard to be reinforced from the right side, drawing from where the army was virtually unopposed to add pressure to the central core.

It seemed like hours passed, and neither side was making appreciable headway when the sound of trumpets from the opposing force announced a retreat. Whistling sharply, she signaled her own retreat, with a combination of trumpets and signal flags. She waited for the commanders' reports on the keep.

The three people she appointed commanders made their way up to the rooftop. She no longer remembered their names after seventeen years, and this lack of clarity only made the shame of not recalling them all the greater.

The woman that was appointed over the left vanguard shook her head. "We're not pushing them back on the left. They stand steady on that side."

From the commander of the centre came, "With the flanking maneuver from the right, we were in a great deal better position than we initially thought. If the same situation comes down again, then I think we can swing to the left as well and relieve the pressure on them."

On the right, "We were virtually unopposed on the right side – I suspect they weighted things into the centre and protected their left, but didn't have enough manpower to protect the right in the same way."

Tyrielle nodded with each report. "Tell your men to fall back and get some rest wherever, however they can. This is not going to be a short battle, nor an easy one," she ordered. The three saluted her – for the last time as it would turn out – and retreated back down the keep steps with their orders. Evening was coming on, and Tyrielle did not expect another assault before the next day. She would keep vigil and be cautious, but night battles, especially against a fortified position, were among the riskiest of endeavours in war.

She looked down into the courtyard and saw Myr just as he put the finishing touches on another ward. The chill white light of magefire died down and inscribed into the wall where it had been, was a runic-inscribed circle.

A few hours passed, and with the edge of night coming on, Tyrielle looked over the valley again, a sudden movement amongst the enemy army drawing her attention. The army parted and a solitary figure, clad in armor, neck to foot, steel armour with ivory and scarlet embellishments, stalked forward. As it drew closer, she inhaled sharply and blew a whistle to get the attention of the signallers. A series of wide gesturing hand signals later, she ordered the archers to open fire on the man striding across the battlefield. Not just any man, but the Divine Emperor himself.

Arrows began to rain through the darkening

sky, but as each it approached its target, it was incinerated in a tiny flicker of white fire. The army began to rouse itself and as they began to take up defensive positions, disaster struck.

Dozens of beams of magefire lanced out all at once and swept across the shoddy defensive lines. Screams began to erupt from the men touched by the magefire. Tyrielle's right side began to itch, even though she had not yet been struck by magefire. And the Emperor strode forward, every projectile vaporizing before it came close to striking him, any man that stood to face him took the brunt of two or three separate blasts of magefire before a smoking corpse would collapse. A few probing beams even struck the walls, but, protected as they were by the wards, they stood strong and resistant to it.

It was like something out of an alchemist's lair. Tyrielle remembered once seeing an alchemist take a bullseye lantern and shine it into a faceted crystalline ball, and a million million beams of light struck out into the darkness of the room. This sweeping array of magefire was reminiscent of that. Tyrielle ducked as a lance of magefire launched towards her position on the keep. Skittering across the floor, she descended into the keep and sprinted through the floors to make it to the courtyard, where Myr and Myr's brother, Zarik, stood.

Whistling again, she called out the signal for retreat and directed the forces to flee as best they could, while she stood with the other two waiting for the Emperor. Harsh moments passed and Tyrielle drew her sword, more to ease her nerves than any need to be ready.

And the Emperor showed himself at last.

Words passed between the Emperor and Myr, words that were distorted as if through a waterfall, as Tyrielle forgot exactly what was said, and the Emperor then raised his hand. First one beam, then a second, a third, a sixth, a tenth, launched forward. And each beam of magefire was met with a ward constructed in the air of magefire itself, spinning runic circles that seemed to devour the white fire entirely. But the onslaught was endless, and massive. Zarik pulled Tyrielle away from the growing conflagration that was once the courtyard of the Anderwyn winter home. The Emperor saw this, and threw his other hand in their direction, launching another dozen barrages of white fire. Myr extended his hand in kind and wards began to form, but not fast enough. Tyrielle screamed in agony as she caught the brunt of the blast on her right side, Zarik shrewdly scooped sand from a nearby barrel, extinguishing the magefire.

Soon Myr had the magefire under control. But the Emperor advanced, and with every step, an additional lance of magefire launched out, only to be answered by Myr's wards.

Myr screamed at Tyrielle, "GO! Leave this place, flee. Be safe!" And Tyrielle refused to go, but she was weakened by her injury and Zarik was able to drag her away. Her last sight of Myr before the magefire overwhelmed him was of his cocky grin looking to her, as he called out, "I love you," for the last time. The next sound she heard was a brief shriek of pain, and then nothing, as she and Zarik fled into the night.

***

Tyrielle awoke from that dream with a start, gasping for air, her scars itching like mad from the fresh memory of the burning. Arzades turned to her with an expression of alarm and he crouched over her.

"Are you alright, mother? It's just a dream, just a dream," he said soothingly as she began to calm down, nodding in response, "What was it that so alarmed you? I've never seen you like that," he added.

"Just... remembering something, pup. Something dark and terrifying, and I wish I hadn't remembered it. Why don't you get some more sleep? I'll take what's left of your watch, and then my own."

Arzades nodded and took his mother's place in the tent next to Renias to sleep, and Tyrielle stood awake, watching the night, trying not to scratch at the maddening itch of her scars. She could not bear looking at the fire, so she looked out into the darkness, breathing deeply and suppressing the urge to weep in remembrance of the last time she had seen Arzades' father.

Chapter 12

The night's rest completed for the four of them, they sat in comparative silence around the remnants of the campfire as they snacked on the little food they could. Renias shared the fruits of his scrounging, producing a stock of root vegetables that required a quick wash, as well as some edible mushrooms.

"You learn a lot in the army if you ever want to eat anything besides the bog-standard rations they give out," he mentioned when asked about his natural awareness.

Tyrielle consumed her food silently, thoughtful and troubled about her dream from the night before. It had been years since she had endured that dream, endured remembering the events that led to her fleeing into the night while unknowingly pregnant.

Unwilling to focus on the pain of the dream itself, she chose to remember Zarik, who had escorted her to a group of friends in the Free Cities before he returned to the Empire himself.

"To make trouble," he had said in his traditional grumble of a voice.

Arzades watched his mother carefully, still concerned about her reaction in the middle of the night and further concerned by her silent thoughtfulness now.

"Mother, is..." he started, interrupted by her looking up with a levelled stare. Falling silent, he nodded and returned his attention to what was left of his breakfast. The last one to finish, he gathered up the slabs of bark and the like that they had used for improvised dishes, much to Damarion's discomfort, and tossed them into the small fire pit, scattering the fire to extinguish it before standing up to find the tent already packed up and the bedroll furled and ready to go.

Damarion leaned against a tree while he was waiting for the clean-up of the camp to conclude. "I do have some dishes and the like we could have used, you know," he called out, to a mostly noncommittal response. Shrugging, he looked off to the northwards and the growing light upon the plains of the southern Crosslands. "If memory serves me right, we won't make it to Elard not today or tomorrow, but instead the next day. Then we'll know for sure if they're simply following my path in reverse or not. I just wish we could get some horses to make this all easier," he said, mostly to himself, but Tyrielle noticed, pausing briefly before continuing in her closing of the camp as she replied,

"We'll get horses in Elard – no place between here and there will have riding horses worth their salt and I don't want to waste our time with draft or farm horses," she said.

"With what monies? I barely have much coin left, and I don't know about you, but I somehow doubt that you were able to save enough for four or five good riding horses working in a small backwater village, in any capacity."

With that, Tyrielle finished packing the tent away and reached into the pouch at her side, and pulled out a handful of coins. Where earlier she had only produced a pair of silver from the pouch, this was instead a full handful of gold coins, stamped with the Imperial sigil. Pursing his lips and nodding in response, Damarion replied, "I stand corrected. With that and a bit of luck, we'll definitely have horses in no time."

With the camp packed up and the fire put out, the four of them set forth once again. Renias took the lead still, followed by Tyrielle, leaving the two young men jockeying for position at the back of the group. The bickering was less than half-hearted, more akin to the rivalry of siblings than of comparative strangers to each other, and it earned a smile from Tyrielle. That was one thing she regretted from the style of life she had chosen for herself and Arzades – it left little room, if any, for companionship of one's peers. And these two, for their slight physical differences – Arzades was a bit taller, with lighter hair and darker eyes, clearer skin – could be brothers in how they acted. Tyrielle was not sure how much of this was Arzades constantly craving attention from his peers or not, but whatever the cause was, she decided that it would be, eventually, a healthy thing.

In the long run, she considered, it might even be something necessary. They would not always be traveling like this, on the run, or in hiding. Some day they would have to settle down, and it would be easier for Arzades to settle down if he already had some idea of what to expect from his companions. If he decided to live in a city, that would be a lot of sudden socializing that he would not be prepared for. Tyrielle's thoughts whirled with these considerations, strategizing out her son's life, before she came to realize what exactly she was doing in planning out her son's entire life for him. Doing much the same thing her father had done to her. Taking a deep breath, she shook her head to dispose of the troublesome thoughts and continued her steady march behind Renias, who set a kilometer-eating soldier's pace. In moments they made it back to the main road and set off northward along it.

She considered the man in front of her, who's life had been so ruthlessly uprooted and discarded by the events only a short time ago. Clearly he was competent, as shown by the ease with which he carried the axe and the state which the axe was still in after being buried in a box for so long a time. But he was still mostly an unknown quantity. And it was not exactly like she could ask him for a sparring match – in terms of weaponry, the match would not reveal anything, as any fight between a sword and an axe is fated to not last long.

"So, soldier: where did you serve in your time?" she asked, probing for information to add to her planning capability.

Moments of silence passed as the quartet continued marching, before he finally responded. "Mostly up north on the border, but also near the Free Cities and along the Emerald coast. Never saw out and out combat with another nation, but lots of tiny skirmishes. Worst one was on the Emerald coast. Pirates came down and raided the one town on suspicion of a Kingdom paywagon coming through. Came in hard and fast and there were only three squads left to face them by the time we were able to square off. Earned a commendation that day," Renias said quietly,

Tyrielle nodded, unseen, in response. "Any person serves long enough, they have a story like that to tell," she replied in commiseration, earning a scornful laugh and a nod from the blacksmith. The next few kilometers passed in relative silence, beyond the noise that Arzades and Damarion made trading stories back and forth – Damarion doing the lion's share of the talking.

"So what's yours, then? Assuming you have one and didn't just luck out of your own proverb," Renias asked in turn.

Tyrielle paused for a moment in thought, remembering back to the dream of the night past. Shivering, she shook her head. "Yes, I have a story to tell. But I'm not ready to tell it yet; I hope you understand what I mean," she said, to which Renias turned to look at her a few moments before nodding and returning his gaze to the road ahead.

"I understand. I didn't go into greater detail about the day I earned a commendation for a reason, after all. Things happen. Things that you're not proud of, things that cause you pain, things that you just don't want to talk about with just anyone. That you won't be ready to talk about for a long time," he said, his voice cracking slightly as he spoke. Tyrielle nodded again, and the kilometers passed until the nightfall came again.

This time there was not an errant tree grove for them to shelter in, so they made camp in the leeward side of a small hill to shelter from the wind. They made a small fire using grass for tinder and lit the wood branches they had brought with them from the night before, set up the small tent and the bedroll, and settled in for the night.

***

This time when Tyrielle awoke with a start, it was Renias who was awake on his watch.

"Sleeping well, I take it?" he said, poking at the fire with a longer stick. Shuddering with heavy breaths, she nodded and crawled out of the tent and sat across the fire from Renias. Long moments passed in silence between them, with only the crackling of the fire to distract them from the outside. Internally, Tyrielle's burns itched distractingly enough, but she pushed down the urge to scratch at them as Renias began to speak.

"I didn't want to tell too many people at once, as this takes a lot out of me. The last time I told this story, it was to Alari the night before our wedding. And all she did was take me in her arms and kiss my forehead. She didn't judge me at all. I couldn't have taken it, not from her, and not about this," he said, stirring up the flames of the fire.

Tyrielle nodded and she stood up, moving to Renias' side and sitting down again, closing in so he wouldn't have to speak over the fire. Long moments passed where she saw the memories eating their way through Renias' mind before he began speaking again.

"So the pirates, right? Didn't know what they were doing, didn't know how to take on a proper formation. So they'd just charge us, and we'd weather their charge, beat them off, and march forward. This happened so many times that day that we all lost count, our last remaining officer included. I probably accounted for more than three dozen dead that day, and I *know* I was not the one who killed the most. It wasn't combat, it wasn't fighting, it was slaughter. Pure and simple. Then, the pirates simply fled, leaving behind almost a dozen triremes. By the end of the tally, there were more than a thousand dead. A thousand dead, at a simple fishing village on the Emerald coast. More than that. We were regaled as heroes for protecting the paywagon. But I don't think a single one of us was happy with what that day brought us. I put in for a discharge the next week, and I saw the men who stood beside me in the line do the exact same. For a damned paywagon," Renias emphasized, shaking his head and throwing the stirring stick into the fire. Tyrielle was silent for a long moment before she nodded.

"Thank you for telling me about it, Renias. I can't say I know what that's like, to know that level of disgust with yourself, your actions, and your chosen career. But know that I also don't blame you for what you went through that day," she admitted, shaking her head.

"Does that tell you enough about me to know what use I'll be in a fight?" he said, ruefully grinning at her through the flames.

Tyrielle snorted and nodded back to him. "I'm not surprised you knew why I was asking. But yes, it tells me everything I need to know. That you're reliable. That you're resolute in the face of danger. That you're willing to do hard things when hard things need doing," she retorted. She saw a half smile develop on his face before the gloomy attitude reasserted itself, and the night returned to silence. After an hour or so, Renias stood up and took Tyrielle's spot in the tent, leaving Tyrielle to the silence. She looked away from the fire, the use of the fire as a centrepiece no longer needed and so, she dismissed it from her sight.

***

At noon the day after next, the walls of Elard came into view. Tyrielle inhaled deeply and turned to look to Arzades, forcing a smile. "Do you remember the last time we were here, pup?" she said, falling in step beside him for the last leg of the trek, "It was quite some time ago, but you weren't old enough to really see what a city was like then. Now you are, and I hope it doesn't overwhelm you too much," she teased, just as much to divert and needle Arzades as to distract herself from the sense of foreboding the growing walls instilled.

Arzades viewed the walls with some degree of trepidation, Damarion with boredom, and Tyrielle and Renias both with cautiously guarded excitement. At best, Elard was the next stage of their journey, where they would be really prepared and ready to confront the duo they were chasing down. At worst, Elard would be a trap, where they would find Iron and Tempest ready for them.

Chapter 13

The outer portion of the city of Elard was almost exclusively homes, not businesses, but here and there could still be seen a crowd partaking of a shop's wares. Tyrielle led the way now, and she passed the buildings on the outside of the wall until they passed through a great gate in the wall itself.

After stepping to the side to confer for a moment with one of the gate guards, she returned to the group to say, "Alright, I've got directions to an inn for us to stay at. Nothing too fancy, but it usually has the space available, the guard says. Come on."

A few moments later, they found themselves standing before a fairly rickety building. Moss was growing up on one side of the building and ivy across most of the rest of it. A mostly faded sign presented an image of a flying bird-like creature and the words, while mostly faded, could still be read as "The Gryphon", with a word completely obscured from the middle of the sign. Pushing forward, Tyrielle led them inside. Once inside, the smoky atmosphere made itself plain. It was not too bad, but smoke was definitely present, causing a wrinkling of the nose and a consideration if this was the best place to stay after all. Inside, within the smoke filled common room, were several people at different clusters of tables, all of whom had paused in what they were doing to turn and look at the newcomers.

Just before the group had a chance to reconsider their options, a boisterous call from behind the counter called their attention, "Greetings, fellows! I bid you welcome to my establishment, The Gryphon! Please, come in, make yourselves comfortable. Excuse the smoke, my grandson decided that today would be a great day to help out in the kitchen. What can I get for all of you?" called out an affable older man, clearly fighting the grey in his hair with whatever dyes could be found, but for all that carrying a youthful attitude for what his apparent age must be. Behind him through an open door, the kitchen could be seen, and the cries of children and a toddler giggling as a woman scolded someone for their interference.

Tyrielle could not help but half-smile, and beckoned the others to follow her over to the counter. She leaned on the counter top and surveilled the options behind the tender and owner, before raising an eyebrow. "You've got some pretty high-quality goods here for being such a comparatively out-of-the-way establishment, friend. What's the story behind that?" she asked, probing the owner for information as if fencing with him.

"Ah well, I inherited this place from my grandfather, as my father had no call to run it, bless his soul. And grandfather put every last copper penny earned from this place back into it as an investment. He never saved a single coin, I don't think, so we have some of the highest quality beds, we have a number of rooms always available, and yes, our stock of liquors is some of the greatest in all of Elard. I reckon The Gryphon could even stand toe to toe with The Lion's Rest or The Unicorn, in terms of quality. But alas, one thing you can't do with money is up and move an entire building. So while we have regular customers, returning guests, and the rare wanderer in such as yourselves, we don't make enough to thrive. We don't get the truly high paying guests, and as such, part of our stock is wasted. Wasted on these dregs!" he called out to the crowd jovially, earning a chorus of boos and dismissals in return, "We merely make enough to survive comfortably, and for that, I'm thankful to the Twins," he said, miming a gesture of lifting something from his chest and kissing it before returning the nonexistent item.

"Sounds like we've found the perfect place

to suit our needs then. Ideally, we'll only be here one night, but we may need multiple in the case of disaster," she added in caution.

"Ah, fair enough, fair enough. The standard rate is a silver per room, with free breakfast, but all drinks and all other meals must be paid for individually."

"Excellent, that sounds fantastic. I'm... assuming... that your grandchildren will not be helping make the breakfast?"

"Ah, no. They're only here after breakfast and during the day that their parents are out working. The only meal you have to be worried about them helping with is whatever we serve for lunch. Which today, would have been some roast goat, but *someone* kept setting the spit too low and we ended up with a side of charcoal instead," he called out, the grin taking any malice from his words whatsoever.

"Then we shall take three rooms. The big guy and myself will take one each, and the two boys will bunk together," she said, turning to the group to ensure the details were fine by them. Renias nodded without any hassle, and Arzades and Damarion looked at each other and shrugged in mirrored unison, "Yes, three rooms. One with two beds."

"Well then, if you'll follow me, I'll get you set up with your rooms and the keys," the older man said, coming out from behind the counter and grabbing a large bundle of keys on a ring, and led the way to a partly concealed side door. "Do you have any preferences for location of the rooms?"

"Preferably together in a cluster, but beyond that, anything will do," Tyrielle replied easily.

"Excellent, excellent. Then I believe the rooms you're looking for are right here on the main floor," the innkeeper stated, opening two doors on one side of the hall and a single room on the other, revealing two rooms with a single bed each and a room with two beds respectively. Handing over the three keys used to Tyrielle, he bowed low and swept a hand out to the side, the remaining keys jingling in his hand. "I leave you to your rooms and return to my post as any loyal soldier," he announced, whistling a soft tune.

Before he turned a corner to pass out of sight, he turned back to the group. "If you should need something from me and I'm not at the bar, you can ask for me, Arjax, or my wife, Leonina, and we'll do our best to get to your needs as soon as possible," he said, then passed from view.

Tyrielle smiled for a moment, a full warm smile before she beckoned them all into one of the rooms. Handing over the other solitary key to Renias, she gave the double-room key to Damarion. "Alright. Now, to business. We have a great deal to do today, and if we don't get it done today, we'll lose time because these are all things we need to do. If we had been able to get all this in before leaving Arvil, we'd have done it then, but we didn't have the chance."

"Renias, you're the least likely to be recognized by Iron and Tempest if they see you, but you still know them well enough to describe them or find them. I want you to canvass the city and see if you can find them or find where they went, from where, how they went. You know everything we need to look for," she laid out, to which Renias nodded.

"I'll head out now, then."

"Be back shortly after nightfall at the latest. And be careful. I know what they've done to you, but you won't avenge anyone if you get yourself killed recklessly and to no end."

Renias nodded again in affirmation before he stepped out of the room and disappeared down the hall. Tyrielle then turned to the two young men. "Damarion, I want you to pick up horses for our journey. As a nobleman, you'll have at least some idea of what to look for in a good horse. Make sure we don't get any nags and that'll be good enough. Five of them, specifically, though a sixth would be better."

"I'll need money, of course. My father's name doesn't count for anything this far into the Crosslands."

"You'll have it when we're done here. I'm going to track down a store for provisions and other supplies we'll need for the journey going forward so we're not reliant on scrounging and sleeping routines in order to get by," she said as she started parting out the money into three separate piles.

Arzades whistled softly at seeing all the coins laid out, as intermixed with the silver and copper were several golden coins as well. "Oh yes, you didn't see these when I showed Kyrie before. Yes, I've had gold all this time. I buried it with the sword, what use was gold and silver going to be in a small village like Arvil?"

Arzades shrugged in response, nodding. "So, what do you want me to be doing, mother?"

"Ideally, I'd like you to do nothing, stay inside and keep out of trouble, pup. But that is neither practical, given we have needs at this precise moment, nor is it fair to your first real time in a city. So, this is what I want you to do. First things first, take that sword," and she gestured to Arzades' back, "to a blacksmith, a weaponsmith ideally, and get them to grind out the edge and polish it. Then get yourself a sheath of some kind for it. After that? Just stay out of trouble. Enjoy yourself if you can. And be back here by shortly after nightfall at the latest."

Arzades paused, the obvious excitement sending a ripple throughout his body. "I'll do my best to abide by your rules. Anything else?" he asked.

"No, that's it. Damarion, you stay out of trouble too. We need all the hands for this task that we can get, and I would hate to explain your fate to your father when I return to the Empire," she admitted, handing out two roughly equally sized bundles of coins, keeping a third for herself. "Now, get out of here. We have work to do."

The two young men left, leaving Tyrielle alone to herself for a few moments. She tied the last bundle back to her waist and stood up, stretching before she left the room herself. Moving back to the common room, she sidled up to the counter and leaned on it again. Calling Arjax over, she asked, "So where would one go if they were looking to get set up for a long trip? Looking for a tent, some bedrolls, and provisions, anything else you can think of, kind innkeeper."

"Well, as a matter of fact, if you go back towards the main thoroughfare and turn to your right, you'll find a place called 'Tooley's Goods'. Tooley is my son and if you tell him I sent you... well, he won't give you a discount, but at least he won't try to scam you." Tyrielle chuckled softly, pushing off of the bar.

"We should all be back by nightfall, innkeeper. When do you close up for the night?"

"Oh not until the third or fourth hour past nightfall at the absolute earliest, and I'm up for at least a couple hours after that, anyways, so you can be let in. Older folk don't need to sleep as much, don't you know," Arjax drawled as he wiped clean a glass and returned it to the shelf.

"Yea, I've been noticing that myself as I get on," she replied ruefully, half-smirking and heading towards the door.

"Oh, pssh. You're a spring chicken compared to me, so don't you go giving me that 'getting old' spiel," Arjax called out. Tyrielle chuckled in response and found her way back to the outside of The Gryphon. She turned around before she got too far, and acknowledged what seemed like rickety construction was in fact solid; it was just slapdash additions to a much smaller building that caused the building itself to look like it was on the edge of falling over. Satisfied with her assessment, she went off to find Tooley's Goods and to see whatever else this city held for her.

Chapter 14

Sure enough, Tooley's Goods was right where Arjax described it to be. It was a smaller building, but there was evidence of a basement or cellar construction in its humble presentation. Tyrielle pushed her way through the door, setting a chime to ringing, and took a quick look around the interior. There were racks of assorted random goods, anything from small decorative items to chairs hanging on display. Satisfied with the scope of the goods available, she worked her way through a labyrinthine maze of waist-high shelves to make it to the counter, where a younger man with bright orange hair waited.

"Welcome, welcome, welcome. I haven't seen you around before – this is Tooley's Goods, and I am Tooley. What can I help you with?"

"Ah, thank you, Tooley. I'm looking to stock up on supplies needed for a journey, it'll be lasting... oh, two weeks should be long enough. We have horses as well, so we'll need feed in addition to food. We also need three bedrolls, a tent large enough to hold two people, and a mess kit, and if you happen to think of anything else, I'll be happy to pay you for that as well," Tyrielle laid out, leaning on the counter and drawing imaginary tally marks for emphasis as she spoke, Tooley nodding along the way. Rapidly he pulled out a sheet of paper and a charcoal stick and scribbled down notes as she finished speaking. Nodding twice, he looked back to her.

"And will you be waiting for this order, picking it up, or what?"

"Your father sent me here; is there any chance we could have these things delivered to The Gryphon?"

"Ahh, of course, of course. Thank my father for me when you see him for sending you my way – I'm always glad to support his customers. Means he gets more repeat business, after all. I do quite well for myself – better location for the store and all – and with mother and father willing to look after my daughters and my son for me, I don't have to pay for the care of a nurse or nanny, while my wife is off singing with her bardic troupe, she earns her own money as well. Oh, my apologies, you must be busy if you're preparing like this for a journey," Tooley paused and worried, to which Tyrielle shook her head and half-grinned.

"Don't worry about that. I've got nothing but time today. Finding you was a real boon in my favour. When planning this day out and sending my fellows scattered to the four winds to get everything accomplished, I expected my task to take all day, to find someone that would be reasonably priced and still have everything I need."

"Oh, don't you worry about that. I don't have everything you need, but I have enough to turn a profit and I can send one of my runners," he said, gesturing to a pair of scrawny boys in a corner, "to another store to pick up the remainder. Then we bundle it all up and bring it on over to the inn after business is done for the day. We'll charge you then, and it's easy as that. Any questions or concerns about what we'll be up to?"

Tyrielle shook her head. "No, seems simple enough. Nice and clean – I take it you've done it this way before?"

"Oh indeed, indeed. Many a time, don't you worry about that none."

"Well then. Now that the lion's share of my day is taken up, do you have any recommendations as for entertainment in the city?"

"Oh, Elard's not got much in terms of strict entertainment, so to speak. But if you go on up to the main square, there's a dozen or more kiosks and stalls there to peruse, and on top of that, there's usually someone playing music for their supper by the fountain. My wife's normally up there when she's not on tour, like she is now. About this time she should be in... Freeman's Post, I think, or around there abouts."

"Oh, she travels far then. Must make good money if they range as far as that. Especially in these days," Tyrielle responded with some surprise, drumming her fingers on the countertop.

"Oh she does, she does. Every time she comes back, we arrange for a new supply of stock art goods from local creators, sell them at cost to those who come in shopping around, so that word of these creators gets out and about a lot more easily. Twins willed it, one of our sales led directly to the artist being tapped by the Lord of Elard himself, and from there, it's only a short jaunt to the capital, a haven for the arts and artists like him. Anyways, I'll let you get going now, have yourself a grand old day," Tooley replied, waving Tyrielle off.

"I'll leave you to your business, kind Tooley. I'll work my way up to the main square and see what there is to capture my attention."

Chuckling softly, Tyrielle left the shop behind her and walked out into the afternoon sun. Looking both ways, she shrugged and turned right, heading up to the main square to see what distraction she could find for herself.

***

Damarion left the inn at a brisk pace and found himself on the main thoroughfare of the city of Elard with barely a clue as to the direction he needed to go. Rolling his shoulders, he set off towards the main square of the city, eager to find a person to ask for directions and to get his task done. Once in the open square, he paused to look around at the hustle and bustle of the city of Elard. Not as impressively large as Citadel Kyrie, but still impressive in its own right. It definitely was not so provincial as to earn a look down his nose, that was for sure.

Music played and a soft folk song rang throughout the square as he surveyed the different businesses present. A lot of food and craft wares were located here, as well as a storefront teeming with exotic animals. Damarion wandered the kiosks, pausing at an apothecary's stall. "Pardon me, kind madam, but I was looking for some directions and hoped you might be able to help me out here," he called over to the aged woman behind the counter. She turned to look directly at him, and he noticed she was wearing a facemask covering her lower face.

"Ahh, noble sir, welcome. Directions, you say? I'm sure I can help you out, if you help me out a little bit,"she croaked out, gesturing to the various and sundry wares before Damarion. Damarion shrugged and picked up a single jar, labeled 'Panian wort'.

"I'll take this, madam, if it'll help you out some," he replied, showing it to her to reveal what he had picked up.

"Ah, the wort, very good. Two silver coins for a jar that size. A little pinch in your food or water will help you stay awake much longer into the night. Much more than a pinch, and you'll start to sweat like you had moved to the Marsh Realm. A lot more, and well, you'll have enough time to dig your own grave and crawl in. You'll have the energy to do it, too. So, noble sir, what were those directions you wanted?"

"Ah, excellent. Yes, I'll take this, then. I'm looking to acquire a number of horses. Knowing that sometimes they require treatment by an apothecary, I figured this was the best place to start asking around," he said, gingerly slipping the jar into a sack and flipping over a pair of silver coins to the apothecary who snatched them out of the air like lightning.

"Ah, horses, yes. I know several places for horses. What kind of horses are you looking for?"

"Riding horses, specifically. Maybe a couple of pack horses too. But riding horses are the priority."

"Ahh, well then. You'll be looking for Ebilard's stables. He's just on the north end of town, easy to get to. Head for the north gate; you'll see some stables on your right hand side. That's Ebilard's. He usually has fresh stock in from a farm out in the hinterlands, good for riding, good for stowing things away on. He'll sell you tack and gear as well, for cost if you're buying horses. Ebilard's a good man, always quick to call on me if he thinks he has a sick or injured animal, and I patch them right up. Don't you worry about getting a nag from him – it's been an age since he called on me for animal aid."

"Sounds like just the person to go talk to. My thanks, madam. I'll be off now," he said as she wandered back to the far side of her stall, nodding a farewell to him as she tended to several plants and one small kettle over a tiny brazier. Wandering off, he oriented himself and walked up to the northern gate of Elard.

Before too long, Damarion found his destination – a well-appointed stable with a decent fenced in area beside it, a boldly coloured sign above the entranceway proclaiming proudly "Ebilard's". Stepping inwards, the smell of animals hit him. Not overwhelming, so they must clean the stables fairly often. He looked around quickly, seeing better than a dozen animals plus more in the fenced in area outside.

"Hey youngster, what can I do for you?" he heard a voice call out. Looking around, it took him a moment to spot the ancient man in a wheeled chair in the corner. Briskly, the old crow wheeled himself out to face Damarion.

"Yes, unsurprisingly to you I'm sure, I'm looking for horses. Four at the minimum, looking ideally for six. Willing to pay in gold as necessary," he replied, looking down to the old man.

"Ha. I like you, young'un. Yeah, I got a batch of horses that'll do you well. If you want six of them, it will cost you twelve gold coins."

Wincing, Damarion opened the pouch and

counted. Eight. Eight the second time, too. Sighing he looked to the old man, thoughts whirling through his mind. "Well, old fellow, I was directed here by a friend of yours, an apothecary who's set up their get-up in the main square. I can't tell you how heartened I was to hear that your stable does such a brisk business with an apothecary – I'd hate for it to become known that it was extremely common how often she was over here, tending your animals that should be for sale," he countered, looking for any weakness that would let him bid the old man come down in price.

"Two gold coins each is a fair bargain sir, and I wouldn't deign to sell animals that were less than full-weathered and ready to run in a heartbeat. But I tell you what – ten coins and your silence that we see the apothecary around here, and I'll throw in the tack at cost to you," replied the old man. The longer he was close to Damarion, the older the old man seemed. After consideration, he decided the old man must be easily twice Tyrielle's age, if not more.

"Aha, but oldster, I already know you sell your tack and gear at cost when someone's buying horses from you. Surely you can do a bit better than that."

"Cursed old hag, she told you that, did she. Fine, son. Last offer, eight gold, tack at cost, for six horses. Six premium horses that otherwise could be going to the noble families of Elard. They come here for their stallions, don't you know."

"Done! Eight gold, and I'll make it a ninth gold in silver for the tack and gear. Do you know The Gryphon Inn?"

"That's young Arjax's place, right? Yeah, I know it. I knew it back when it was called the Golden Gryphon even."

Damarion mouthed the word "Young," shaking his head. Compared to this ancient old one, Arjax could probably have been a youngster. "That's the one. Can you have the horses brought there?"

"I can do that for sure, young'un. They'll all be kitted out for riding and ready to go if need be, so if you don't want them for riding tonight, you'd better take care of them and take all that gear off them for the night. I'll be mighty angry if I sell you horses, only to have them maltreated. This is Ebilard's, not some nag shop."

Damarion laughed in response. "Don't worry oldster, we'll be good. We might be using these horses for a while and it wouldn't do for them to collapse under us just because we were lazy. I can see you've a stock of fine animals. I'll tell you what, just to make the sting of our deal a bit less, I'll overlook it if you send us one or two animals just a bit under peak performance," he said as he handed over a positive handful of coins leaving his pouch much lighter than when he started.

The old man stared up at Damarion from his chair with lopsided, bushy eyebrows. Then he burst out belly-laughing, a surprisingly loud sound coming from his aged frame. "I was right, I do like you, young man. No, you argued well. You argued dirty, but you argued well, and I'll honour the bargain. Just don't let people know how much I charged you for them," he laughed out, pointing and wagging an angry finger at Damarion. Damarion nodded and waved a farewell to the oldster, before pausing and looking back to the old man. "Ebilard – it is Ebilard, right?" he asked, getting a nod, "How *old* are you?" he asked as a follow-up.

Chortling, the old man paused as if thinking for a moment. "Not a day younger than ninety three, young man," he answered, causing Damarion to choke for a second and shake his head.

"Whatever you're doing, keep it up. I expect to see you here next time I'm in Elard."

Snorting a laugh, the old man wheeled himself back into the stable corner where he had been waiting for customers in the first place, and Damarion found himself wandering back to the Gryphon Inn, with six coppers left in his pouch.

***

Renias found himself at the west gate of the city about the same time Damarion was buying horses. He was quietly lurking near the gate, and whenever someone would pass just slow enough to obviously be idly taking their time, he would approach and ask if they had seen an incongruous pair, a slender, almost effeminate individual accompanied by possibly the largest man in all of existence. As of yet, he had received very few answers, and all of those had been in the negative. Sighing, about ready to give up, he went up to ask the new gate guards, the shift having changed over in the time he had spent here asking questions.

"Excuse me, dear sirs, I don't mean to interfere with your important work here, but I'm wondering if you could help me. I'm looking for some people."

The guards looked at each other and shrugged, one leaning back against the gate house, the other turning and approaching Renias. "Alrighty, fellow. Describe'em to me and maybe I'll have seen them, maybe I haven't. I just don't know yet."

"One is a small individual, almost a young adolescent. The other is a huge beast of a man, nearly silent. The other one would do all the talking."

"Don't know if I've seen a pair like that."

Renias looked the guard up and down, noting the cocky grin on his face and a smirk on the guard behind the first and nodded. "I see, I see. Then perhaps something that would help you ease your troubles – once you're off shift of course?" he said, slipping a pair of silver coins from his purse, over to the guard.

The guard pursed his lips thoughtfully and nodded satisfactorily, slipping the coins into a hidden pouch on his person. "I didn't seen them, but the guards on shift this morning did. I only know they're your pair because it was Big Toth that was on shift, and apparently this guy dwarfs Big Toth."

Nodding in acceptance, Renias thanked the guard for his service and turned back to head to the Gryphon Inn. He made it as far as the main square, as he paused to look around at the city. Technically he was born just a few kilometers north of Elard, so he had been to the city numerous times, and it was in Elard that he registered to join the army. It had not changed much in the meantime. Still only one wide street, the others being clusters of twists and turns. The main square was where all the action happened, and even now it seemed like this was where everything happened. The multiple kiosks, the storefronts, the crowd around the fountain... even now, the crowd was there, in the middle of the day. Some there for business meetings, some there to socialize, and some there to listen to an ivory-robed woman sing a beautiful, heartbreaking song.

With lots of time left in the day, he found his way over to where the woman was singing. She was beautiful. More than that, in a crowd of beautiful people, she would stand apart. And her singing was heartbreaking, to the point that Renias felt his eyes water. His mind turned to thoughts of his family and the brief time since they had passed, and the waters broke over as he listened to the woman sing.

Memories of fishing trips with Alari on the rivers near Arvil. The summer afternoon that she told him she was pregnant with Marik. The night he was playing with little Marik in the forge when Alari came in with a shovel and started shovelling snow away, only to pause and tell him she was pregnant again, this time with Eillel. The first time all four of them had gone out fishing together, when Renias threw Marik into the river, to the laughter of all. The weddings, two weeks apart, of both Marik and Eillel.

But the memories he dreaded never rose from his subconscious mind. Only the happier ones, the ones he missed rather than feared, came to his imagination.

Untold minutes passed and the song finally closed, to which a single man applauded once before falling silent. The woman turned and saw Renias, crying against one of the fountain's statues. Descending to the ground of the square, she walked over to Renias, offering a simple smile and wiping his tears away before she turned around and walked away to the east. Stunned, Renias waited until she was out of sight before he turned to one of the nearby folks and asked, "Who was that? She sang so... sadly."

Shaking his head, the man he addressed shrugged. "Don't know. No-one I know knows. She showed up here three or four days ago and started singing. The same sad song every day. Never at the same time, avoiding any troupes or troubadours that might come by. Don't know what the song is, either, but you're not the first to be affected like that," he replied.

"It was... something. I don't know how to say it."

"Aye, you're not the first one flummoxed by her either. But you feel better now, don't you?"

After a momentary pause, Renias thought about it. The memories still stung, were still fresh, but they no longer felt crippling and debilitating. "Yes, yes I actually do," he said, acknowledging the change, "Has no-one ever followed her?"

"No man. It feels like... it feels like it would ruin something, you know? No-one I know has dared follow her, so no-one knows where she comes from, goes, none of it."

"Hmm. That's... that feels right, you know. Like the magic would be gone if the mystery was."

The other man nodded, and Renias stood up. Feeling invigorated for the first time in several days, he rolled his shoulders and returned to the Gryphon and retired to his room to await the return of the others.

Chapter 15

Arzades paced around the small room. Five steps, turn. Five steps, turn. A couple of steps, then a detour around the furniture in the corner to end up back where he started. He did not plan for this to be the outcome of his day, nor exactly did he expect this to be the outcome of his decisions. Wincing in thought, he paused to consider what his mother would think. Tyrielle would not be pleased, to say the least. At best, he was in for a verbal thrashing. At worst, the next time he had practice, he would be facing off against her, and she would be far less than kind. Sighing, he continued his pacing around as he considered the chain of events that led to his being arrested and thrown in the Elard city jail.

***

It really seemed simple enough. His only actual task was to find a blacksmith and get him to work his skills on the sword so that it was ready to see action. So the first stop was the gatehouse that they entered the city through to find himself someone to get directions from. The city guards there seemed approachable enough, so waiting respectfully until they were done questioning a merchant who was bringing in a wagonload of goods, he approached the closer guard, a woman close to him in age it seemed.

"I beg your pardon, miss, but I was wondering if you could help me out some?" he asked, smiling at the guard in a bid to be personable.

"Hmm? Oh, sure. Wait, didn't I see you come through about an hour ago or so, asking for directions to an inn?" she responded, leaning her pike up against the nearby wall and crossing her arms, leaning herself against the wall beside the pike.

"Oh, yes. That would have been my friends and I. We found the inn, so you and your compatriot there have our thanks. But I've got a chore to run in the city, and I was hoping that you might be able to help once again."

"Sure, sure. What do you need?"

"Directions again. Looking for a blacksmith. Specifically one that deals in weaponry and repair thereof. I've got a family heirloom that requires some looking after before it's in proper shape."

"Oh, is that what you're lugging around there? Looked like a sword the first time through, but weird way to carry it. Makes sense that you're looking for a smith then. Well, if you want the official line, I can tell you Chorrol's smithery is the place that the guards are subsidized to take their gear to. He does good enough work, more than serviceable and his prices are good."

"That sounds particularly good to me right now... but what about the unofficial line?"

"Well, that would be my cousin Rithen. Now now, I know it sounds like I'm recommending family for work, but Rithen does particularly good work, good enough to be tapped by the nobility for crafting and repairs. If he's got the time, he'll polish out all the nicks and dents in mere moments and get you on your way without any trouble whatsoever."

"Well, that sounds even better. I'd like to have some time to myself to get out and see the sights of the city," which got him a smirk from the guard, "And if he's at least skillful enough to do the job right, and fast? Then it marks off all the needs I have. Again, my effusive thanks for your assistance!" Arzades proclaimed, palming a silver coin from the pouch at his side and flicking it to the guard, who caught it, biting it quickly to assure herself of it's quality before stashing it in her pouch.

"No no, thank you, kind sir," she replied, standing upright, "To find Rithen's smithery is pretty easy. He's two streets east off the main square.

Just look for the building that looks like a forge," she directed, before taking her pike back in hand and returning to her post at the gate itself.

Arzades smiled and turned around, heading down the street of the city. He rubbed his jaw slightly, mouth unaccustomed to some of the words he had decided to use, but sounding educated in this particular case felt like it would serve him better than being some country bumpkin. Which he of course was, but sometimes it served to be smarter than you actually were, his mother had taught him. It was like carrying a reputation of being undefeatable in combat, it led to you facing fewer opponents and the ones you faced were already half-defeated before you began, so his mother taught. And even from his inexperienced perspective, the lesson made a great deal of sense.

Finding himself in the main square of the city, he paused to gawk. Gawk was definitely the right word, as there were as many merchant kiosks here in the main square of Elard alone, as there were houses in Arvil. The real scope of the city hit him then and he took his time wandering the square, stopping at every stall, at every countertop, even at the bards tuning their instruments and singing songs that Arzades had not heard before. Breathing deeply of the scent of the city, masked with spices and plant smells from the nearby kiosks, he resolved to return to the square once his task was accomplished. Freeing himself from his reverie, he oriented himself and wandered eastward, passing even more storefronts that led from the square in that direction.

Two streets later, and there on the corner was a forge. Smiling in gratitude to the nameless guard, he wandered over to the forge and stepped under the awning, looking around. It looked similar to Renias' forge, yet different. Tools were in different places, the forge itself was slightly different, but they were all there. What was majorly different was a selection of hanging swords along the back wall. The sound of ringing hammer strikes beat into him from the corner, where a wide man and a pair of youngsters were taking their turns hammering a red-hot length of metal. One of the youngsters looked up and nodded in his direction, the wide man muttering something and barking an order for the kids to continue hammering. He then turned to face Arzades, and approached him across the forge.

The first thing that struck Arzades was the glossy white orb that occupied the smith's left eye. The second thing that struck him was that he was looking up at the smith. Craning his neck, up. "Well? Speak up, young one. I have not got all day – what are you here for?"

"Well, I've got a sword I need cared for. More than I can care for it on a roadside. And I'd prefer to keep it – it's a family heirloom," he replied. Wordlessly, the smith held out a hand, and Arzades unslung the bundle from his back, unwrapping the sword his mother had buried. Whistling softly, the smith took the sword, examining it swiftly, looking along the blade, lifting it and looking from the hilt down the length of the blade, running a hand over the gems in the hilt and crosspiece, all in the span of a moment.

"Gonna take more than a bit of work. I could do it fast, but you'd lose material in the blade, moreso than otherwise. It'll take some grinding, polishing. I'd hate to do more to it, because it would probably mean breaking the baby down and remaking it," the smith said appreciatively.

"I'd rather not take that step if at all possible. It's the only gift I got from my father, and had to wait sixteen years to get it."

"Ahh, understandable, understandable. Then the grind and polish it is. I've got a pretty full docket, so it'll take a little bit of time to get to it and get it done. You okay with that?"

"How long are we talking here?"

"Just tomorrow morning. I'll have free time while waiting for the boys to get in and get the forge back to full heat, so I'll get it done then. Good enough?"

"It'll have to be. We'll be on our way out of town early tomorrow, and we can pick it up then if need be."

"Sounds good then, young sir. Anything else I can help you with?"

"Don't suppose you provide sheaths and belts for weapons here?"

"As it turns out, we do, we do. I'll get one

that's as close to this blade as possible for you, and have it ready for you tomorrow as well."

"Excellent! Now, to the important things. How much will this cost?"

"I could get this done for a gold coin, but you don't need to pay me until you come pick it up. And if you take longer than a week, I reserve the right to sell it off. It'll make a pretty penny to the right noble, for sure. Punishment for wasting my time, don't you know."

Arzades paused in thought, weighing his options. He could go and find another smith, even ask Renias if he'd be willing to do the work with another smith's tools, but eventually, he decided to take the risk. There'd be no way it would take longer than a week to get back to the smith, and if they did, retrieving one sword would be far from the first thing on their minds.

"I'd rather you not, but I understand. I'll be back first thing tomorrow," Arzades answered, getting a nod from the smith and, business concluded, Arzades turned with a hasty step back to the main square to take a look around. A breeze washed over him and it carried with it the scent of cooking meat. Swiftly he found his way to the source, a storefront selling meals over the counter, and doing a brisk trade. Joining the line, he craned his neck to look around. It looked like a side of beef was being carved and served on a simple clay platter with a slice of bread. Soon enough came his turn and, after forking over the copper coins for the meal, he wandered off to look around some more. The options were nearly overwhelming as he finished off the chunk of beef and started snacking on the bread. Noticing a pile of the clay plates nearby, he added his to it, and wandered over to a vendor selling fresh fruits.

He was far from the only person perusing the stall. He looked over and saw a trio of children looking over the stall, alternating between glances at the vendor himself and the different arrays of fruits. Becoming engrossed in the different colours and shapes of the options available, he barely noticed when the children burst into action, each grabbing an armload of fruits and sprinting away. Unfortunately one turned and sprinted into him. In the ensuing chaos, he ended up carrying one of the fruits the child had stolen. He heard a shout from the vendor who looked after the children in one direction first, and then the other, and then noticed Arzades. "Hey! You! Thief!" he loudly proclaimed.

A million thoughts whirled through his head at once. Foremost amongst them was his mother's voice, "The one thing I told you not to do!" Tyrielle shouted inside his skull.

Hearing a new sound, he looked to the side of the square where a cluster of guards were rushing over. A pair went east and a pair went west, chasing after the children, and a pair approached Arzades directly. In a panic, Arzades flung the fruit at the guards and took off to the southwest, down a narrow street. Breathing deeply and remembering

141

his mother's words for running, he took long, loping strides, trying to keep his breathing as steady as possible. Hearing the guards in pursuit, he began taking turn after turn after turn.

Until he came to a dead end. Cursing the Twins, he spun around to choose another direction, to realize the guards had already closed off the exit. Breathing deeply, he took steps backwards until he was against the wall directly. Bracing himself to sprint forward and burst through the guards, as was his only hope, he launched himself forward, and felt the odd sensation of time beginning to slow down. The movements of the guards were muted and slow, as were his own. Looking past the guards, he saw a dark-cloaked man look down the alleyway towards him. A man dressed almost entirely in black and other dark colours, with maybe a dozen weapons visible on his person. The man turned and passed from sight, and with a rush, time resumed its frenzied pace. The guards snagged him from his distracted stupor and brought him to the ground. Swiftly he was tied, lifted back to his feet and shoved forwards. "Come on, kid, off to the jail with ye," one of the guards said, as the other prodded him forward with the butt of his pike.

"I don't suppose you'd believe I was in the wrong place at the wrong time?" he asked, earning a dark look and a short snort from the guards.

"And I'm the Queen of the Marsh Realm," one of them replied sarcastically.

"The Marsh Realm doesn't have a Queen,

they're ruled by..." he managed to get out before getting clouted by the pike. Groaning, he turned back and started walking.

"Any other stupid remarks ye'd like to make, young'un?"

"Yeah, can't help myself. Can I at least talk to my mother first?"

The second bash was, if anything, harder than the first, causing Arzades to limp now as he was goaded onwards. Approaching a solid grey building, they led him inside. Led him past a desk with a secretary at it, down a set of stairs and a hallway, into a selection of cells that laid open. Untying his restraint, they shoved him into a cell, slammed the door behind him and locked it swiftly, turning back before Arzades interrupted them.

"How long do you plan to keep me here?" he asked, genuinely, the snark taken out of him with that second clout.

"You'll be up to argue your case inside a couple of days, and if there's any justice, you'll see the inside of the cells for a couple of weeks," one of them said, chuckling darkly as they left the hallway.

A couple of weeks, Arzades mouthed, slamming his head into the bars of his cell. Renias would not be happy. Damarion would not be happy, though he might be amused.

But worst of all was going to be facing his mother down after this.

Chapter 16 - Second Interlude

He drummed his fingers on the arm of the throne to a beat only he could hear. Even when others were present in the throne room, it was silent until he spoke to them. But there was always a lingering tune, a song that played within his mind. He knew the source of it too, but in knowing, he knew that there was nothing he could do, lest he lose everything.

He sat above a house of cards, he knew, playing subjects against each other so they were too busy playing power games instead of massing together to try and overwhelm him. Not that they really could anymore, not without a signal to rally around nor an exceptional mage to protect them, but it was an annoyance he did not want to have to deal with. Not when he was busy with other concerns.

Reminded of that, he lifted his hand and massive waves of magefire encircled the throne room. Soon they suffused so much of the throne room, it was hard to see anything past them, any of the pillars, the entrance, nothing. It was part of the reason why the only decoration within the room was the scarlet carpet that contrasted the ivory colours of the rest of the room. And he was careful to avoid igniting that with his fires. As they reached the very ceiling of the chamber, he closed his hand into a fist, and the magefire condensed itself into weird geometrical designs, half-triangles and half-squares, circles and ovals blended, other equilateral shapes, all twisting and bending within and onto each other, forming a three dimensional ward, but a ward that served a very special purpose.

A purpose only he could know, or the entire house of cards would fall apart.

Speaking of falling apart, with the ward created and circling the room, he sighed and let himself relax as much as he could and still produce the ward. Amongst other things, the ward gave him peace from the siren song that so compelled him otherwise. Lifting his hand higher, he oriented the ward to obfuscate the entrance to the throne room to the best of its ability. He thought back to that day nearly twenty years ago when he faced off against Myr Anderwyn, the mage he thought might finally be able to defeat him. But Myr was not yet good enough, and his power had only grown since then.

Struggling to remain composed, he remembered the last thing Myr did was to protect his wife and to speak words of love with her, in a scene that nearly broke his own heart. Nearly. At that moment was when Myr's attention wavered just enough to allow one lance of magefire through his multiplicity of wards, and the whole thing collapsed. He saw to it that Myr did not suffer for long – it was the least he could do – and he did him the respect of not pursuing the traitor into the night, though he certainly could have, and without a mage to protect them, it would have only been a matter of time and miniscule effort.

His willpower waning, he clenched his fist harder, so hard the nails began to dig into the skin. The ward remained stable, and his mind remained clear. He knew he would have to attend to the various nobles eventually, but the first one to go had to be Kyrie, and that would take some delicate work. Well loved by the people, respected by the other nobles, any direct effort to move against him would only provoke insurrection, and he could not have that. There must be stability, at all costs.

He knew the pettiness many of the others got up to, especially the other dukes, knew their inclinations and their practices, but he was powerless to stop them as long as they continued to squabble against each other. Remove one too precipitously and the others would get uppity either out of fear or out of boldness. It was a complex web he weaved amongst them, and as much as he hated much of what went on, he needed the stability.

The ward began to wobble, and he shuddered. There was limited time left before he would have to become the implacable monster once more. He relished these times of peace and independence, to allow him to think and consider everything instead of merely move pieces on a chessboard. To that end, he now considered the task he had set Tempest towards, allowing them to take their brother with them. They were to observe the Kyries and seek out any weaknesses that might be exploited. He hated doing that to the respected Kenzen Kyrie, but if he did not oust all the nobles, there was no point to ousting any of them. And the other dukes needed to be purged, lest they mistake license to do what they want as indifference to what they are doing.

Breathing deeply, calmly, there was one last thing that needed to be accomplished before the ward went down. Something that none living had seen or heard, nor would they, if he had anything to say about it. It would only ruin his credibility as an implacable monstrosity, an all powerful archmage beyond the scope of any mage standing today.

He wept.

Wept for all the losses that happened to preserve the state of society in the West. Wept for those who had lost loved ones, both young and old. Wept especially for the young who never had their fair chance to live in the world. Wept for those who would die in the name of his unspoken crusade.

He wept for himself.

Moments passed as he began to control himself, and the ward wobbled again. This time it collapsed and fell apart, and he braced himself. Within his head there was a brief moment of screaming, screams of rage, of effort, of impotence. He shivered as the screams filled his head, before the same ethereal sensation as always, a hallucination of a pair of invisible lips kissing his forehead, and the screams fell silent, to be replaced by a wordless song.

Restored to his implacable self, he reached inside his coat and reached for the letter which Tempest had sent in report. Reading it once more, he pondered the boy, Damarion, and where he might be heading to in such secrecy. Tempest reported that they would be following, and would report back once they had dealt with the boy whether it was peaceably or not.

Lifting his head to stare into the ceiling of the room, he ticked off possibilities until scant few remained. Damarion was looking for someone. Someone who lived not in Kyrie lands, but instead someplace further east. Knowing Kenzen and knowing the Kyrie attitudes, this someone would be antithetical to the standing order of the West. He smiled briefly. Exposing this might be the very wedge he needed to oust Kyrie. Because there was only one person that Kenzen would seek out with enough desperation to quietly send his son out to look for them. One person that he would want to come to him, that would be aligned with the Kyrie interests. He only awaited Tempest's report.

Damarion was looking for the traitor.

Chapter 17

Tyrielle looked outside the small window in the room to the dark sky. Night sky. And Arzades was not yet back. It took her several deep breaths to calm down enough to approach this rationally. Renias and Damarion both had returned and were just killing time in the common room of the inn, whereas Tyrielle had retired to her room, first to check to make sure Arzades had not snuck in somehow, but also to reduce her visibility. She did not think that there were counter-agents at play in this chase, but when it did not cost her anything to be more subtle, why should she not?

She held up both her hands to weigh the two - comparatively equal – possibilities. Either Arzades had gotten distracted and was still out and about within the city, partying, celebrating, just generally making a nuisance of himself and he would be back any time now... or he had somehow gotten himself into trouble. And if that were the case, there would be no telling when or if he would be coming back to the inn. First thing tomorrow, she resolved, she would go out and begin seeking signs of his passage. She would prefer tonight, but between the low visibility and the simple fact that there would be minimal people out to ask after her son, she decided that the course of wisdom lay in tomorrow. Besides, maybe a miracle would happen and he would return in the middle of the night whilst they were all asleep.

Stepping out of the room and returning to the common room, she discovered that, besides a single person who – she had been informed – was also staying the night there, they had the common room to themselves. She reversed a chair and straddled it facing the table. "No sign of him, then?" she asked the two, to a pair of shaking heads.

"No, no-one's come to the door since he locked it up a couple of hours or so ago. Not in the room I take it, then?"

Tyrielle shook her head. "No. Boy's gotten himself in trouble somewhere, I can feel it. I'll be going out to look for him in the morning, dig him out of whatever situation he's found himself in, and be back here as soon as possible. The two of you, I want you to stay here, coordinate the supplies and the horses that will be arriving. With any luck, we'll be able to leave when it's still morning."

The pair nodded and Damarion got up and headed in the direction of the rooms, leaving Renias and Tyrielle alone. Renias took a long draw from his mug and looked over to Tyrielle. "I take it you're against us leaving without you if the time draws on too long?"

"Definitely. I understand you have your reasons to want to catch up to them, more than anyone save *maybe* myself, but if we learned anything from Arvil, it's that we won't be able to take them down piecemeal. It will take all of us, and it will take a plan that we must execute perfectly or even it will fall apart."

Renias sighed and stood up, knocking over an empty mug. "I suppose you're right. I don't have to be happy about it, but you're right. If it takes longer than noon tomorrow, I'll bring us and our tack and gear over to the west gate, so that we can still be best ready."

Tyrielle agreed with a nod and stood up herself, the two of them retiring back to their rooms. She watched him close the door behind him and heard the clacking sound of a heavy lock settling, before she pushed open Damarion and Arzades' door to see Damarion fast asleep. Nodding, she closed the door again and entered her own room. She kicked off her boots and laid down on the bed, staring up at the ceiling, willing sleep to come to her quick and easily.

***

Arzades' night, on the other hand, was not as restful. The cells, which had been mostly quiet during the day, were now filled with a cacophony of criminals crowing at the guards and at each other. Not that Arzades was lying in bed trying to sleep anyways – shortly after nightfall, the guards had opened his cell and deposited a wild-haired and disheveled woman, reasonably young but still old enough to get tossed in the cells with other criminals.

"Well, there went my luxury room," he drawled, causing the woman to snap her head around and stare at him for a few moments before snorting. She moved over and sat down on the bed, shuffling around to make herself comfortable on what must be a straw-filled mattress.

"Ain't seen you before, least not 'round here. What are you in for?" she said, her voice fine and smooth, belying her appearance. It caught Arzades off guard a bit, before he moved over to lean against the exterior wall by the head of the bed.

"Didn't do it, but they seem to think I stole some fruit."

"Ha, no surprise there. They don't care 'bout investigating on the spot, waste of time they say. But makes sense. They love to catch the small fries – usually easy work, and they get the most money out of it. Guards here turn a tidy bit of business in collecting fines to let people out."

Arzades snorted and the two remained silent for much of the rest of the evening, going into the night. As night rose in the sky, the woman scratched her head and yawned, curling up small on the mattress, patting the mattress behind her. "Come on kid. Lie down and go to sleep – there ain't going to be much to do until the morning," she beckoned.

Arzades coughed for a moment, caught off guard. "I mean... lie down with you? I... uhh...." he spluttered and stammered, earning a soft, melodious giggle from the woman.

"Boy you really are a country bumpkin, kid. Don't worry, it's not like that, unless you want to pay me. But, suit yourself," she said, shifting up against the wall and leaving plenty of space on the bed. Arzades stood and paced around the room for several more hours before finally deciding to take the woman up on her offer and slid onto the bed beside her, facing away from her and trying to keep some space between them, futilely.

***

Tyrielle was up earliest of them all, and was already ready to go out into the morning before Arjax rose up and unlocked the door. She set herself a brisk, albeit conservative pace, heading first to the southernmost gatehouse, where they came into the city. Pausing for a moment while they finished up with someone at the head of a wagon train, she then approached the young guard closest to her.

"Hello, I was hoping you might be able to help me. I'm looking for someone – my son. He's a little taller than me, brown hair, carrying a wrapped bundle on his back."

"Ah, yea, him. I know him, he came here asking for directions yesterday. Poor kid get himself lost?" the guard, a woman from the sounds of it, asked.

Tyrielle shrugged in response, "I don't know, but he asked you for directions? Where to, maybe I can pick up his trail there."

"Oh I sent him off to Rithen's smithy. Main square, head east two streets, can't miss it."

Tyrielle nodded her thanks and flipped a silver coin over to the guard and headed off before she saw the guard's response to the coin. She briskly moved up the main thoroughfare and past the main square heading east, easily enough finding the smithy. As she approached, she noted instantly that Arzades had been here – the smith was in the forge, currently working on the Anderwyn sword. "Pardon me, sir, but my son came by and dropped off that sword yesterday," she said, breathing deeply at her exertions so far that day.

"Hmm? Oh yes. I can see the resemblance. I'm sorry but the sword's not ready yet..." the smith stated, before Tyrielle raised her hand.

"That's fine, that's fine. I'm looking for my son – do you know where he went after visiting you?"

"Ahh, well, he went back towards the main square. Beyond that, I do not know, miss. I'm sorry," shrugged the smith, returning to working on the blade, a shower of sparks flinging into the air. Tyrielle nodded her thanks and returned back to the main square. She paused for a moment to catch her breath and to let the sounds, smells, and sights of the main square wash over her, seeking in the sensations a clue as to where Arzades would have gone. Cursing softly, she started with the closest kiosk and worked her way around in a circle, visiting the storefronts as well. Nearly an hour passed of inquiries and questioning before she found her way to the fruit stall where Arzades had been the day before.

"Oh yeah, that thief? The guards ended up getting him got and dragged him off to the westward jail," the fruit merchant chortled, "They'll fine him within an inch of his life, if he can even pay it. If he can't, well, it's prison time for him."

"Thief," Tyrielle mouthed. Well, that certainly explained why he did not come home last night, but she never expected Arzades to become a thief – he had plenty of money that she sent him off with, so something must be up, some discrepancy somewhere. Nodding her thanks to the merchant, she harassed a different merchant for directions to the closest jail, and found her way there in the span of a few minutes.

Entering the grey building, she approached the desk and cleared her throat to get the guard's attention, who was busy scratching in notes with a quill in a ledger of some kind. A moment or two passed, and he set aside the pen and folded his hands in front of himself. "And what can I do for you, citizen?" he inquired.

"I believe you have – wrongly or rightly – arrested my son. I'd like to free him," she said, leaning on the desk.

"Ah, well, that's as may be. Do you know how we do things here?"

"I assume I pay some sort of fine and we're good to go?"

"Not quite. If you pay to free him before trial, you pay for the full cost of the crime times a factor of ten, plus a two thirds administrative fee," the guard rattled off, with the same effort as a practiced chant. Tyrielle felt her coin pouch and nodded.

"He looks a bit like me, minus the scars. Taller, brown hair, brown eyes. Young."

"Ah yes, the kid. He's down in cell one, with the prostitute. Led the guards on quite the chase, from what I understand. Anyways, crime of stealing fruit, 3 pieces were missing at the end of the crime. Two coppers a piece becomes six coppers, which becomes six silver for the fine, and plus the administrative fee, that's one gold even."

Tyrielle paused, briefly considering the merits of waiting until the trial, but shook the thought from her head. Producing a single gold coin from her pouch, she let it click onto the desk. "There's the gold coin. Now, may I have my son?" she asked, biting the words off one by one.

The guard nodded and pocketed the coin, lifted a set of keys from the wall behind him and led the way down towards the cells. When they got to the cell, she spotted her son and slammed a fist on the bars. "Wake up, pup!" she ordered, snapping.

***

Arzades awoke instantly to the sound of his mother's voice. He looked down to realize he had rolled over in his sleep and was now thoroughly entwined with the woman from last night. Holding his breath he carefully disengaged himself and extracted himself from the bed, moving to the door as the guard unlocked it. He opened his mouth to speak and a glare from his mother silenced him. He looked into the cell one last time to see the woman waving to him with an idle hand and a smirk on her face.

Tyrielle remained silent the whole way back to the Gryphon, to see six horses, loaded up with gear and provisions. Nodding, she turned around and grabbed Arzades by the collar and heaved him against the wall. Wisely choosing to not resist, Arzades felt the air whoosh out of his lungs as he slammed into the wall. And then the lecturing began.

"One thing. One thing I told you not to do, and you had to go and do it, go and get into trouble. Stealing, no less. No, I don't want to hear it, if you weren't guilty then you shouldn't have been there in the first place. You're smart enough to be able to figure out when trouble's coming. That's when you get out of the way, not stand there looking gobsmacked and getting pinched for a crime."

"And another thing! If you were getting pinched for a crime, don't make the guards run and chase you down, that's just going to make them ignore anything you might possibly have to say. Like, I don't know, maybe 'I'm innocent'? You just made the guards angry and cost us a gold coin, of which we have precious few left."

"And one last thing – who was that you were so cozy in bed with? It didn't look like nothing, it looked like a fair bit of something, in fact. That's the absolute last thing we need, you getting attached to someone. Especially someone like that, someone you know absolutely nothing about? That's just absolute idiocy – what if she had been some agent of the Empire? What would you do then? No you wouldn't, because at best you'd have been dead."

Concluding her tirade, she exhaled sharply through her nose, screamed within a closed mouth, and poked Arzades in the chest, hard, once for each point before she went into the inn to pay off Tooley and collect the last of her belongings in the room. Arzades turned to look at Renias and Damarion – Renias had absolutely zero expression on his face, but Damarion? Damarion was definitely amused by something.

Arzades sighed and moved to one of the horses with an empty saddle and began the process of figuring out how to mount the horse – the others sure were not going to help him, and maybe if they were ready to go by the time his mother got out, it would lessen the suffering he would have to endure later.

Chapter 18

The quartet started their ride through the city by passing by Rithen's smithy to pick up the sword for Arzades. Collecting his payment, the smith retrieved the sword and a leather belt and sheath sized almost exactly to the blade and handed it over to Arzades, who immediately set to the effort of putting it on. Tyrielle gracefully hopped down off her horse and moved to her son, silently – angrily almost – assisting him with it. Eventually between the two of them, they got it sorted and Tyrielle remounted almost as quickly.

Arzades, unused to the new weight on his hip, approached his horse carefully. Taking a deep breath he reached up and shoved his foot in the stirrup and swung around, coming to rest in the saddle. He then patted his horse, whispering a brief prayer to the Divine Twins that the animal had not started moving while he was climbing. Looking to Tyrielle and Renias, each of whom was leading one of the extra horses, he nodded. In response, they set off leading the way towards the western gate where Renias had picked up the trail of Iron and Tempest.

As they approached the gatehouse, Renias slowed and called out to the guards, "Ho there, guardsman. You're the same fellow I asked for help from yesterday, are you not?"

The guard leaned his pike against the wall and nodded. "Yes sir, I am. You asked me about your friends and where they went," the guard replied easily.

"Yes, excellent. I had one last thing to ask you before we headed out of the city after them. Do you happen to know if they were mounted? We don't want to unduly tire our horses if they're moving slowly after all."

"Makes sense, makes sense. Let me confer with my friend," the guard replied and moved back to his associate. A quick conference later - the quartet had moved to the side of the street so as to not block traffic - and the guard returned. "Jezray says they were mounted, yes, but the big'un was mounted on a draft horse, so they're not going to be moving too quickly," said the guard.

"Perfect, my thanks to you and your friend. Please, help yourselves to something cool to drink when you're off shift," Renias replied, leaning down and gently tossing a silver coin to the guard, who nodded, returned to collect his pike, and resumed his post.

Onwards the quartet went, passing through the western gate of Elard into the outer city. The attitude was already much more relaxed out here, and Arzades took careful note that there were far fewer guards in the outer city than the inner, and that fact alone allowed him to relax slightly more – not that he planned to stop near any shops in the near future, or the far future for that matter.

Damarion pulled his horse back beside Arzades and matched pace with him. "So, your mother said you were snuggled up to someone while you were in prison?" he asked, curious.

Arzades sighed and looked to Damarion. Realizing that the other young man was unlikely to drop the topic, he slowed down to make it easier to both speak and still control his horse. "It really wasn't anything. She was put into the same cell as me and after we talked for a moment, she went to sleep. I didn't really have anywhere else to sleep, so I took her up on her offer and got into bed. I didn't intend to... get close, not as close as I did, that's for sure. Then mother found me like that in the morning, before I had a chance to disentangle myself from her, and got myself into trouble that way too."

Damarion laughed slightly at that, covering a brief flicker of a different expression that Arzades missed. "Well, at least it's not like you got into any *real* trouble with her, right? Your mother also said she was a prostitute, and you probably could have for just a few coins," he responded gently and slightly speeding up the pace to catch back up with the others, goading Arzades to stay with him.

"One, she tried to get me to pay her at one point, and not knowing how it was going to be, I wanted my first time to be something with a little more meaning. Two, there were no walls between cells, only bars, so we would have been watched by everyone and their brother. Three, I'll admit, there was some... fear, at play, while I was in that cell. Not knowing if you or mother or Renias would be able to find me before my sentencing came up."

"Why didn't you pay your fine? Your mother seemed to take care of that with remarkably little trouble."

"I didn't know that was an option, and didn't even know to ask. Unsurprisingly, this was my *first* time in prison."

Damarion laughed again and fell behind Arzades in line, silent now and thinking. Arzades shrugged and, with his attention back on riding, he picked up the pace again and caught up easily to Renias and Tyrielle. "Mother, I-"

Tyrielle held up her hand to interrupt Arzades, causing him to fall silent. A few moments passed in silence except for the clip-clop of the horse hooves on the street as they finally pulled free of the outer city of Elard, riding onto the proper western road towards Isolis, their next destination. After a span of minutes on the road, Tyrielle turned in her saddle to look at her son. "I'm still displeased with you, pup. But we'll talk more about that when we stop for the night. Make yourself comfortable in the saddle as you can, we'll be riding a while, even some into the night, to make up for lost time. We're about a day behind them, and we don't want to fall any further back," she said, flicking the reins of her horse and setting it to a mild canter. Renias followed suit, and Arzades fell in behind the four horses in front of him as his horse instinctively followed the herd, with Damarion close behind.

***

They set up the camp on the shallower side of a hill that night. Damarion tied off all the horses while the others took charge of different tasks in camp – Renias and Arzades each set up a tent while Tyrielle began attending to supper. It was a silent affair, and Damarion took the opportunity to walk around the hill, looking for anything of interest. He felt a pervasive sense of disquiet, and looked for any opportunity to distract himself.

Back at camp, Tyrielle watched Damarion walk off into the night, shrugged and provided food for the other two. "He'll eat when he comes back to camp," she said, settling down for food herself. As the moments passed, she considered her son. It was clear he was contrite and did not go looking for trouble, but she knew if she did not punish him appropriately, he would never learn the full scope of the lesson.

"Come on, pup. Time for another lesson. This time with real steel," she said, standing up and dusting herself off, moving to the far side of the camp from the tents, drawing her short sword with a steely hiss.

Sighing deeply, Arzades finished off the last of his food, stood up and moved over to stand opposite of his mother, drawing his newly refurbished long blade with a straight edge to it. Taking a moment to look it over, he looked to his mother. "What's the lesson this time?"

"This fight won't stop until you draw blood, pup. That's all."

"But, that sounds needlessly dangerous, mother. Why no-" he started to say, before Tyrielle took rapid steps forward and with a swing and a flick of her wrist, she sliced open Arzades' cheek.

"Come on, pup, you don't have all day," she replied, skittering backwards into a guard stance.

Arzades cursed, brushing his left hand against the cut, coming away with plenty of red. He paused and examined his mother's pose. Nothing struck him as a weakness, so he began to approach, taking advantage of his longer arm and longer blade to launch a probing thrust, only to be batted away by his mother who stepped inside his reach and elbowed him hard in the stomach, launching him backwards and down to the ground.

"Pathetic, pup. You get one more try before I lose my temper on you," she directed, sweeping her arm and sword wide as Arzades got up. Before he got all the way up, however, he dropped the sword and launched himself forward and low before his mother could resume her guard. His heavy tackle took the wind out of her and sent the short sword falling off to the side even as they fell down themselves. Then, a mad scrabble to reach the sword – Arzades reached the sword first but took a foot to the gut as he retreated with it. Coughing, retching, he stood up and faced off with his mother again, who seemed unperturbed to be unarmed. Standing square with her, with the fire at his back and the Anderwyn sword, the only unattended weapon, behind him, he considered how to attack her. Should he fail this time, it would only reflect poorly on him. If he succeeded, he would possibly be injuring his mother, and when they could be catching up to Iron and Tempest at any time, that could be a fatal mistake. Sighing, he winced and felt the cut on his cheek again, and a cocky grin spread across his face.

Seeing that, Tyrielle launched herself forward and Arzades responded by tossing the short sword to the side and booting the longer Anderwyn sword aside as well. Tyrielle crashed into him, knocking him - as he caught her with an arm under hers and a hand on her chest - back a step before she swept her leg around and knocked him over before pouncing onto him. Smirking, Arzades looked up at her. "I win, mother," he said, pointing to the centre of her chest. Looking down she saw a bright red letter, drawn in blood. She paused in confusion and when the realization hit her, she rolled her eyes and slapped Arzades gently on the chest.

"Damn you, and your father both, with the same sense of humour," she cursed, standing up and collecting her sword and sliding it back in its sheath before handing the other blade back to Arzades, who slid it away and took off the weapon belt.

"I think with that, it's time for bed, before I get into any more trouble," he drawled, crawling into the tent quickly as his mother picked up and threw a pebble at him. Looking to the side, she saw Renias grinning on the other side of the fire.

"You're seeming unusually chipper," she replied, sitting down on the ground beside him. He paused and nodded.

"There was a singer in the main square while I was there. Listening to her sing... it made me cry out all the pain. It's still there of course. And I doubt it ever will go completely away, but it's... comfortable now. I can remember all the good things easier now," he said, pausing to think as he spoke, "It was something... something else, that's for sure. I couldn't describe the feeling to you if you paid me."

Tyrielle nodded and leaned back, looking up at the sky, watching the stars whirl by. "It sounds like it, for sure. Sounds like how I feel about Myr, now. It's hard still, and it's been seventeen years, but it's...comfortable is the right word for it," she replied, drawing idle circles in the dirt beside her.

Renias looked up as well, shaking his head. "I don't know who she was. No-one in the square did. But it definitely changed how I felt. How I felt about losing Marik, and about Alari."

Tyrielle nodded, opening her mouth to speak, before spotting Damarion walking back into camp, clutching his arm. "And what happened to you?" she asked, standing and approaching him to examine him.

"I uhh... might have fallen into a berry bush and cut myself on a broken branch," he said, grumbling as Tyrielle looked at the injury to Damarion's forearm. Cursing slightly, she produced bandages and a small bottle of liquid from the packs on the horses.

"This is going to hurt you some," she said, pouring the liquid onto the bandages and then binding the dampened part hard over the injury, eliciting a muffled grunt from Damarion. Tyrielle turned and stowed the medical materials back in the pack from whence she got them. "You'll be right as rain soon enough and it shouldn't get infected," she said, earning a nod from him. He sat by the fire and ate the rations cooked by Tyrielle in silence, before crawling into the tent beside Arzades and laying down to sleep.

Renias looked over at Tyrielle and leaned over, keeping his voice soft, masked by the crackling campfire, "That didn't look like a wound caused by a berry bush to me. Looked like a knife wound," he whispered softly, to which Tyrielle nodded.

"Let the poor boy rest. I don't know what demons he's got haunting him, but harassing him about them won't do any good," she replied, equally as soft. Renias nodded in agreement and got up, clambering into their tent and laying down to rest, leaving Tyrielle to take the first watch. Unwilling to stare at the bright light of the campfire any longer, she faced outwards into the darkened night, plagued by thoughts upon thoughts.

Chapter 19

On the road west from Elard the quartet rode for the intervening days, mostly in silence, though every once in a while Damarion would regale them all with a tale of something he had supposedly done in his short life so far. He was apparently undefeated – he did not count the fight with Arzades – in duelling. He had gone both fishing and pirate hunting on the Emeraldsea, and as a result of the pirate hunting, he discovered in an abrupt hurry that he could swim when an errant turn of the boom knocked him from the ship. He was a lot more self-aware since then, he proclaimed, which earned a smile from Arzades at the very least. Damarion grinned at that and continued expounding on his many adventures.

Arzades, for his part, drank it in. It did not matter to him whether they were true or not, they made good stories and were a good way to pass the time as they traveled the mostly flat lands between Elard and Isolis, which were otherwise unremarkable. They passed several large fields of wheat and other crops to break up the monotony, complete with work crews out in the fields, harvesting, weeding, or otherwise tending to the crops in some way. Politely, Arzades waved to each group of people as they passed, which got him the occasional wave back, but more often ignored in favour of work.

Damarion ushered his horse forward for a moment to harvest a piece of dried jerky from the packs on the spare horses, snacking away as they rode while he waited to figure out the next story to tell. Coming upon nothing, he called forward to Tyrielle, "Should we discuss a strategy for if we encounter them soon?"

"We'll discuss that tonight, since it's unlikely we'll catch up to them today. Although it is possible, so I'll give you all the brief breakdown. Renias, you're going to be our distraction for the big one, Iron, while the rest of us will try to threaten Tempest enough to take them down," she explained rapidly, calling it out loud enough for even Arzades to hear it in the back.

"Sounds basic enough. I look forward to hearing more specifics tonight, then," Damarion replied, shifting his horse back in line until he rode beside Arzades. "How is it in the dust-eater's position, farm boy?" he asked teasingly.

"Hmm? Oh, I'm sorry. You put me to sleep with all your babbling about this and that. What was the question?" Arzades fired back. Damarion snorted a laugh and rode in silence for a minute. When he decided he had been silent long enough, he started singing an old soldier's song he had picked up during the sole pirate hunting trip he had been on:

Well I signed up for the navy
And on the day they came to get me
I sang my farewell to ladies and ne'er-do-wells
And marched off t'see the sea

The first day on the sea,
I had seen all there was to see
I wanted to go back home and leave th' king's navy
But a day out from port we be

The second day on the sea
We came across a pirate fleet
We dodged and weaved and fled the violent scene
But two days out from port we be

The last day on the sea
They caught up t'us on the lee
The pirates took us from port and board and stern
And down in the depths we sleep

His voice sang strong and clear and Renias turned his head to watch Damarion sing the nameless song for a few moments, turning back before the end, his fingers drumming along to the familiar beat. Arzades applauded gently as the song came to a close and Damarion responded with as much of a courtly bow as he could manage from the saddle. Tyrielle smiled and clapped as well, watching the two young men for a moment before she turned her attention back to the road.

The next few miles passed in silence except for the occasional neighing of the horses, the spirits of the quartet high as they rode along. Renias raised his hand suddenly, calling for a stop.

"What is it?" Tyrielle asked, looking around before spotting the disturbance, "Ah. Smoke. We should check it out – anything out of the ordinary is of interest to us right now," she said, holding up her hand to judge the distance of the smoke, "We'll ride up and picket the horses before we go in."

The others nodded affirmation and they pursued the column of smoke that lay beyond a low hill. "Arzades, you stay back where you can see both us and the horses," Tyrielle ordered before moving forward, the others following. At the crest of the hill, Arzades stopped while the others continued forward to a scene of carnage.

Seven charred bodies lay around a scorch-mark on the ground. Tyrielle approached carefully, surveying the bodies. They were obviously all deceased, but she was looking for other signs.

Renias on the other hand, approached the ground and looked for tracks. There were a jumble of footprints, likely belonging to these poor saps – military folk from the looks of it – but he did spot a deeper footprint than it was likely for any of these people to have made. If there was a lighter set of footprints, he did not see them. They went off to the south, where they came from. Following the tracks, he found them leading to a pair of horse tracks, where they rejoined the road and continued west.

Returning to the scene he nodded to Tyrielle, who stood up from one corpse that still had licks of white fire along its body. "It was them," Tyrielle proclaimed to the two, to which Renias nodded.

"They were here, for sure. I followed the big one's tracks back to where they kept their horses. They're still following the road at least."

"Why did they kill these soldiers though? Six men and a woman, dead for what? Do you think it's maybe a warning?"

"Warning to whom? They shouldn't know anyone's chasing them."

"I don't know, then. Damarion?"

The young man started from a reverie instilled by looking over the scene of the massacre. "Hmm. I... don't know. Maybe they're doing it just in case. Maybe they have orders to do something like this. I don't know. The Divine Emperor often issues some... enigmatic commands," he replied.

The trio wandered back to Arzades and together they remounted and turned back to the road, Damarion filling Arzades in on what they found. "And it was definitely done with magefire. Your mother found one body with fire still touching the corpse," he explained, with Arzades shuddering.

"With all this slaughter being done at the hands of ones wielding magic, I'm not so sure I want to learn this," he replied, flexing his hands in the air at the thought. Damarion nodded for a second and they rode in silence before he replied.

"It's a tool, like any other. Like a sword, an axe, a hammer, any of these could be used to kill, and a great deal easier than magecraft – you don't really need to learn any special trick or talent to kill with a physical tool. I'd say it's better to be a mage than a swordsman – if nothing else, you can learn wards that prevent certain things from happening. Like magefire itself, for instance," he said, stroking his chin and rubbing his fingers afterwards.

"I suppose that's true. Wait, how do you know so much about magecraft, anyways?" Arzades asked, puzzled for a moment since Damarion had not shown any inclinations towards magery in their time together.

"Oh, didn't I mention it already? Well, let me tell you about the year I spent at the Academy Arcana Majora," Damarion began. Tyrielle and Renias both rolled their eyes, and Arzades grinned and settled down in the saddle to listen.

***

The story was long and bore many details that did not ring quite true, but enough information was there that it could not really be argued that Damarion *had not* been to the Academy. But it lasted well into the evening and when night fell, the time to set up camp was upon them again. Like an elegant machine, they all set to their tasks within moments, setting up tents, bedrolls, and the night's meal to cooking on the fire.

When the food was ready – in this case, a chunk of roast beef – they all settled in to eat in silence. Tyrielle spent her meal looking up at the sky and the stars, remembering happier days long ago, sitting and eating with a different Anderwyn. Renias spent his meal staring into the fire, remembering the hearthfire of a home that now stood half collapsed and empty.

When the meal finished, Tyrielle called for everyone's attention. "Alright. So, there is no clearly defined plan to take on these two. Ideally we'd take time to study them before we engage, but we may not have that opportunity. So, using a classic strategy – divide and conquer. Renias, we need you to occupy Iron while the rest of us deal with Tempest, because it may take a while to actually kill Iron. We don't want to try and take him out while enduring magefire from Tempest. So we must eliminate Tempest first."

"Do you have any particular ideas as to how to do that? I caught them by surprise last time, but we can't count on that again," Arzades interjected, to which Tyrielle nodded.

"Surprise will be of only momentary gain. Take advantage of it if you can, but don't count on it turning the tide for us. I'll go in first, straight in. Damarion, I want you to come from my left side, and Arzades, I want you on the right. I hope to fight them during the day, because there is one trick that your father taught me about magefire. There is a critical second between when you start to conjure and for the fire to ignite, where you can see a black smudge in the air. If you can spare the attention at *all*, disturb that smudge with something. A rock, a knife, anything but yourself, because Myr told me whatever disturbed this smudge – where the magefire will come from – will be destroyed, or at the very least damaged beyond repair."

The others nodded and Tyrielle returned the gesture before standing up. "Now, to sleep. We'll hit Isolis in the midafternoon. And please note, this is regarded as a holy city, so they're a little touchier when it comes to their laws," she said, looking hard at Arzades, who wilted under her glare. Renias stayed out while the others adjourned to their respective tents, to sleep the night away.

***

Tyrielle was awoken by Renias for her shift on watch and stood to take it calmly. She paced around the camp to ensure all was in order; she fenced with an imaginary opponent; she sat and played games of strategy and warfare with herself;

and she got for herself some of their supply of jerky to munch on while she passed the time.

She was not too worried about catching up to Iron and Tempest any time soon; since they had decided for some reason to indulge in a massacre, it was unlikely anymore that they were taking their time in their travels. So tomorrow, they would have to up the pace in order to catch up at all. Tyrielle was only worried about Arzades in that matter, since he had the least experience with riding and a hard pace might yet be beyond him.

Judging by the shift in the moon that the two hour shift on watch was over, she got up and moved over to the boys' tent to waken Damarion for his shift. When she lifted the tent flap, a wide grin spread over her face as she surveyed the scene. Arzades, curled up most of the way into a ball, and Damarion, wrapped around him with both arms and legs. Tapping Damarion's foot gently, she woke him. Damarion, groggily, slowly untangled himself from Arzades and crawled out of the tent, when alarm came over his face.

"I... uh.... don't suppose you'd care to forget seeing that?" he asked.

Tyrielle shook her head, beckoning him over to the fire for a few moments to chat. "So, you're interested in him, then. Is that why you did this?" she asked, poking at his forearm, causing him to wince doubly, from the physical pain and the reminder.

"It was something about him and the prostitute. It really got to me, and I just felt like I needed it."

"Nothing to be ashamed about. I've known many strong men that lived their whole lives concealing doing such things to themselves. You stand in good company. My husband, for instance, was like that occasionally," Tyrielle explained.

"Please don't tell him. I don't want to put him under any pressure, make him feel bad, or anything like that," Damarion pleaded, to which Tyrielle paused for a while, before slowly nodding.

"At the end of the day, it's not my business who's shacking up with who, if you'll pardon the crudity of the phrasing. And my son is his own man and can make his own decisions. As are you. So, do as you will. Just don't harm him," she requested, dipping her head and then moving to her tent with Renias and crawling in, laying herself down to sleep and leaving Damarion on watch.

Damarion spent the first hour almost entirely staring at the tent he shared with Arzades, before smiling slightly and turning his gaze at last to the star-filled night and his thoughts to futures that might yet be.

Chapter 20

The next morning, Arzades took care of preparing breakfast for everyone. A simple meal of meat and bread, while everyone else packed up the campsite and made ready to leave. Tyrielle took her meal from Arzades and sat down to eat, looking up as Damarion came to get his. She could not help but half-smirk after thinking of last night. It certainly coloured her perceptions a bit. But nothing apparent actually occurred between the two, Damarion taking his food and choosing to remain standing while he ate. Renias grabbed his food as well and the quartet swiftly ate in silence, before packing up even the mess kit, mounting their horses, and riding westward once more.

However, unlike the previous couple of days, Damarion rode mostly in silence, a thoughtful expression across his face. Once an hour had passed like that, Arzades leaned over and poked Damarion in the side.

"Snap out of it, grouch. Sleep poorly, did you?" Arzades asked teasingly.

Damarion grinned slightly in response, "Only because of your snoring, farm boy. Makes me glad we're taking opposing shifts for watches, I'd hate to have to listen to that all night while trying to sleep," he mocked back, getting a snort from his opponent.

"Not my fault I slept so deeply. I had pleasant dreams the first half of the night, and only dozed the rest of the night," Arzades replied, which earned him silence in exchange. Shrugging, he moved back to his original riding position and reveled in the peace and quiet instead.

However, the peace was not to last. Disturbed from his internal reverie, Damarion once more started filling the air with songs and tales of varying truthfulness. Tyrielle smiled at the front of the line, only looking far enough to the side to see Renias grinning as well. Tyrielle returned her gaze to the road ahead, where soon enough they would be seeing the high walls of Isolis.

A couple hours later, her prediction became true as the ivory walls of the city began to rise before them. "Okay, listen up, pup. Isolis is a holy city. This means a few things. One, the priesthood is in charge of virtually everything. If they're not in charge of it, they're in charge of the people in charge. Even businesses operate under the auspices of the church in Isolis."

"I understand, but what does it mean to us? Aren't we basically just passing through?" he replied.

"Twins willing, yes, we will. But that requires us to pass through without incident," she said, looking directly at Arzades, who blushed and looked elsewhere, "To find their trail without trouble, and be on our way. I'm of half a heart to send you around to the western gate to be met up with later, after the showing you made in Elard of staying out of trouble."

Arzades nodded and Damarion rode beside him for a moment. "I can keep him company if you'd like, ma'am," Damarion stated. Tyrielle nodded and returned to the road for a few minutes. Just as Damarion was about to return to his spot, she turned back around.

"No, no. We'll ride together through the city. But you two make sure to stick together, and Renias and I will stick together, and that way, at the worst, we *shouldn't* get into trouble. We'll ask at the south gate if they've been here, and work our way out of the city from there," she dictated.

Arzades and Damarion looked at each other and shrugged as they continued to ride in silence. Passing the boundaries of the outer city of Isolis, it was clear the church did not have much in the way of interests out here. The buildings were falling into disrepair, and it was clear, even through the little that could be seen through the gates of the city, that the inner city did not spend its money on the outer city's disposition at all. Riding up to the gates, they paused as the guards conducted an inspection of their goods. Receiving a raised eyebrow for Arzades' sword alone, they were waved through without any trouble. Tyrielle considered her options and looked down the street leading from the gate. "C'mon, we'll be in trouble if we do something like bribe a guard, even if it's for information. We'll find a shopkeeper, maybe a tavern owner of some kind and ask them."

Even with the party dismounted and leading the horses, it did not take long to find a shopkeeper who admitted they opened extremely early into the day. "Mmm. Yes, yes I open early enough into the day to see the first people pass through the gates in the morning. What can I help you with?" the shopkeeper – a general store owner, as it turned out – said.

"Ah, yes, we're looking for a pair of people, and when we describe them you'll know if you've seen them or not immediately. One's a slender person, smaller than either of the two boys behind me, and does all the talking. The other is a huge brick of a man, likely the largest man you've ever seen," Tyrielle said, sliding a silver coin across the table. The man nodded and pocketed the coin swiftly.

"Mmm. Yes, I know the two. Passed through here late last night in fact," the general storekeeper replied, nodding his head in confirmation.

"Excellent, my thanks to you," she replied, before returning to the others. "So, we've got good news and bad news," she said, running her hand down her chin.

"Good first?" Arzades asked hopefully.

"We're catching up to them," she answered, "And the bad is, they might still be in town, so be on your guard." Leading them forward with a long stride, Tyrielle waited until they got to the open marketplace at the juncture of the three roads that divided Isolis. "Alright. Boys, I want you to go to the northeast gate and investigate there. Find signs of them, or when you don't, come back here. Renias and I will do the same for the northwest gate. And if you find them directly, do *not* engage them, under any means. Even if by some miracle you survive the attempt without us, Isolis' laws don't leave any room for brawling in the streets, and the Divine Emperor himself doesn't have the gold to buy your way out of Isolis' prisons. Wait, watch, and when you think it safe to report back, come back here."

The two boys nodded and led their horses towards the northeast, and Tyrielle turned and, with Renias, went to the northwest gate. Along the way, Renias looked over his shoulder to the direction the boys had gone and back to Tyrielle. "Do you think they'll actually be able to stay out of trouble?" he said, doubt filling his voice.

"Oh, I know they won't, but that's why I sent them to the northeast gate. It leads away from Mereketh and the empire, so it's less likely our hunted would have taken that path. And if I'm wrong, then I'll just have to trust that they can keep each other out of trouble, long enough for us to get there."

"If you say so," he replied.

Finding what seemed to be a fairly well-to-do tavern, they stopped by, tying off the horses and heading inside to find the owner. Behind the bar stood a huge woman, bulky, stocky, polishing off some fine glassware before she set it down to move onto the next piece. Tyrielle leaned on the counter and coughed politely to earn her attention whilst Renias surveyed the rest of the common room. There were only a dozen individuals, but in a strange city with stranger ways, it was best to be cautious in the very least.

The woman turned to see Tyrielle and set the glassware down and, with a swift sideways step, she reached over the bar and grabbed Tyrielle in a bearhug, bellowing "Welcome to the Dusty Maiden, miss! Oh, aren't you just the sweetest thing, what with your sword and all that. Tell me, do you at least know how to use it, miss?" in a deeper voice than expected, and Tyrielle paused before she answered.

"Oh yes, very definitely so. I--" was as far as she got before being pulled into the grand bearhug again. Tyrielle squawked in surprise before being released.

"Oh, I'm terribly sorry for that, I just get so excited when I see a woman taking care of herself and not waiting around for a man to save her. Yes, once again, welcome to the Dusty Maiden! I am Lenallee, the owner and chief bartendress here. What can I get for yous?" the large woman inquired.

"I'll take a beer, but we're mostly here for information. We're looking for some people. Two, in fact, a pair always together. A small person, almost a child in size, and a huge hulking brute of a man, easily half-again your size, Lenallee. The smaller one would have done all the talking, and if anything, referred to the other one as their brother."

Lenallee paused in thought, tossing the dishrag over her shoulder in idle action as she pondered. "Doesn't sound familiar. When would this have been?"

"Last night at the earliest, but more likely this morning," Tyrielle replied.

Lenallee shook her head in a definitive motion. "Certainly haven't passed this way, then. I was watching out there until the gates were closed, and I was awake and out there waiting for people as soon as the gates were open. If they passed this way, they did so under Turam's direct blessing itself."

"Well thank you for that. That tells us much at least. Depending on how things turn out, we might be back this evening. Keep an eye out for our friends, if that's the case?" Tyrielle requested. Lenallee nodded and the pair left, leaving a half finished beer on the countertop. On the way out, Tyrielle raised an eyebrow to Renias.

"What? I was thirsty and you were doing okay talking to the lady," he replied.

"Very well, but no more. We need everyone to be operating at top performance."

"Fair enough, fair enough," he responded, looking around as they got back to their horses. As they untied them and resumed walking back towards the main marketplace, he added, "I don't have a good feeling about this, Tyrielle. If they came in the city, and didn't come this way, then the boys are at risk."

She inhaled deeply through her nose, silent for a moment more as they walked along. "I know, I know. But it's a risk we have to take, now. If we go chasing recklessly after them, it will only force a conflict to happen, if they've encountered Iron and Tempest. So, we go back to the main marketplace, maybe replenish our provisions, and wait for them there. Unless you have a better plan? Because I'm all ears right now," she rebutted, flexing her right hand.

"Not me. I haven't had any good ideas since this whole thing started. Just bad ideas and worse plans. So I'm glad you're along, Tyrielle. I don't think I'd have a hope of doing this without you.

Honestly," he replied, rubbing at the beard that had started growing over the last few days.

Tyrielle half-smirked at the thanks and nodded. "Well, without you, I don't think the three of us would be able to take them on, so your thanks is returned in kind," she replied, and after a while, Renias slowly nodded.

Provisions replenished easily, though their supply of coin was definitely dwindling, they set to waiting in the marketplace for the return of the boys. Noon became afternoon became evening, without any sign of the boys returning, and Tyrielle's worry only increased as the time wore on. "Maybe we should go after them after all, Renias," she began to say, as she saw a familiar sight approaching from one of the side streets. Two young men, leading horses, one calm and mostly composed and the other one as white as a sheet.

Chapter 21

Arzades and Damarion trotted off to the northeast gate of Isolis to begin their questioning, leading their horses. This section of the city, between north district and southeast district was curiously devoid of most forms of merchant. The nearest city leading out this gate was the capital, easily more than a week or more away, so perhaps that was the cause, Arzades thought. Still, there were a few shops that they could stop in and ask at.

"No sir, haven't seen a pair like that at all. Care to buy a sidesword to go with the longsword at your side?"

"No boys, can't say as I have, care for some pickled beets or some potatoes?"

"No."

"Haven't seen'em, no."

"Yes, I've seen them."

Arzades and Damarion were halfway past the shop when they did a double take and circled back to the last of many people they had asked. The person who had spoken up was a sour-faced old woman, one eye seeming like it was permanently closed. She leaned heavily on an oaken cane while tending to her shop, apparently an artisan's showcase.

"Really, old-timer? You're not just pulling our leg, are you? Your compatriots along the street all said they didn't see them. What makes you so different?" Arzades asked, face paused in thought.

The old lady cackled at the two young men. "That's because they only pay attention to the main street for business. In order to keep from twisting up into a pretzel, I go for regular walks around the side streets. That's where I saw them, going into one of the dark taverns, as we call'em around here."

"Dark taverns?"

"Mm, yes. Places that technically are permitted by the church, but there's no... oversight, I guess you could call it. Means they can get away with a lot more than most places, though they have to be careful to not overstep the bounds too much, or they get their license yanked. That one's called the Rotten Hound"

"That... makes sense, I guess? Damarion?" Arzades asked, looking to the other young man, who nodded.

"It's not regular practice for most places, but most places don't have as strict a set of laws as Isolis. I could see that being a normal thing here," the noble replied, which got a nod of agreement from Arzades.

"Well then, I think we know where we're off to next. Ma'am, do you think you could give us directions to where they were?"

"Mmm, of course young man. It's just down three streets and a right turn, and it should be right there on your left."

"Our thanks. Damarion?" Arzades asked as he started leading his horse away. The other young man paused before catching up with little trouble.

"So, how do you want to do this?" he asked as they started navigating the side streets to find this 'dark tavern'.

Damarion paused a moment before speaking, "I think no matter what else we do, I have to stay in hiding. They can recognize me far too easily, especially so because they were sent on this mission to follow after me. So I'll stay outside of the tavern at the very least. What about you? Going to keep me company outside, or go in on your own?"

Arzades considered the options for a moment. "I think I have to go inside. We haven't actually seen them yet, for all that the old lady can *probably* be trusted. I'll go in and do what I can to stay unnoticed – they barely had a chance to see me before they escaped at Arvil, so I should be good."

"You do realize your mother will literally murder me if we do this and something happens to you, right?"

"You worry too much, noble sir. Here, this must be the place. Watch the horse. Oh, and just in case..." Arzades trailed off as he took off his coin purse, made sure to remove all the gold and most of the silver from it and tucked it away in the saddlebags.

"Probably wise. We don't know how dark this tavern really is. Hate to lose all that coin to a lucky purse snatcher."

"Exactly. Wish me luck," Arzades responded before crossing the street, passing the sign decrying the tavern as the 'Rotten Hound' and entering through the front door of the tavern, passing from Damarion's sight.

"I wish you a lot more than that, farm boy," Damarion whispered. He looked both ways and tied the horses off in front of the tavern before finding himself a likely vantage point from which to watch the tavern and catch both the front and side entrances.

***

Arzades stepped into the tavern and the first thing that struck him was that the term 'dark' was perhaps a little on the nose for this business. The walls and furnishings were all constructed from some dark wood or another, and the limited illumination did little to help the situation. For all that, though, the tavern was nearly *bustling* with business, an easy twenty people crowded into the – not quite cramped, but definitely not spacious – tavern. He picked his way carefully towards the bar of the building, hand cautiously on the much-lighter coin purse. The man behind the bar bore a passing resemblance to Renias, but with an extra fifty pounds of fat or so on him. "I have some questions and a mighty thirst, bartender," Arzades proclaimed, sliding onto one of the bar stools.

The bartender swiftly poured a full mug of – ale? – and slid it across to Arzades. "I can help with one of those. Maybe the other if your coin is bright," he grumbled quietly, far less loud than a man of his size would normally speak. Sliding a silver coin across the bar, he took the mug and took a slow drag. A big mistake as it turns out, as he spent the next few moments fighting the urge to bring up what he had just drunk. Swallowing carefully, he set the mug down and edged it slightly further away from him as he spoke.

"I'm looking for someone. Someone that I have reasonably reliable information of them being here, or at least seen here," he began. The bartender motioned subtly for silence, as he looked around the room, ensuring that none were paying attention to the pair of them.

"Yeah, I'm pretty sure I know who you're looking for. They're staying here for tonight, got their horses out back in the shitty little stables I've got. The small one – didn't get a real name, just told me to call them Tempest – was asking after a brothel to blow off some steam. Big one didn't say nothing. Just stood there and stared at me like I were a fish and he were a large cat. So I gave them directions to a place I know about, just a few streets down the way."

Arzades paused with the new information, his mind whirling with thoughts. After evaluating options of pursuing Iron and Tempest versus the virtues of waiting, he decided to claim a spot at a table, sharing with two others that were obviously only sharing a table out of necessity. Calling the bartender over, he paid for a round of drinks to ensure the drunks' cooperation, getting mumbled thanks in response for the ale. He proceeded to psyche himself up to drinking more of the horrendous liquid the bartender called ale and kill the intervening time while waiting for Iron and Tempest to return.

It was several hours later before the door slammed open and Arzades turned just enough to see the door out of the corner of his eye. The not-so-familiar frame of Iron was unmistakable, and right behind him was a slender figure. But behind them was a third shape, a woman, wrapped in a heavy cloak, with shimmering cloth which showed with the occasional motion. His knuckles whitened on the handle of the mug as the trio wandered up to the bartender.

"Tender! I've brought some entertainment back with us. I expect to be undisturbed. And you know what will happen if I don't get what I want, right?" Tempest practically ordered, Arzades straining to listen without being obvious about it. While he looked at his mug of ale, he eyed Iron who had moved to behind Tempest and was surveying the bar carefully. Arzades drank from his mug of ale as Iron's eyes passed over him, and shortly the trio wandered off up a set of stairs and down a hallway from sight. Arzades breathed a deep sigh of relief and looked up to the bartender, who nodded back as he wiped sweat from his brow.

Just as Arzades was getting ready to leave, to report back to his mother and Renias, he heard a woman's scream coming from upstairs. Without thinking, he launched himself towards the stairs and up them. Pausing, he then heard a second scream and rapidly he ran to that doorway, opening it to see the trio. Tempest had removed their shirt, their body covered in burn scars and marks. Iron stood watch by the door, and smoke wafted into the air from a fresh burn scar on the woman's face.

"See, if you had only screamed like I asked in the first place, we wouldn't have had to do that. And now you're going to remember this night for the rest of your life," Tempest said, dusting their hands off and turning to Arzades, "So Iron was right, he did see you, Anderwyn."

Iron leaned over and whispered something softly to Tempest that Arzades could not hear and

Tempest nodded. "Indeed, if the fledgling is here, then so is the mother bird. No telling how many others, but I'm pleased that the traitor is chasing us. It makes the diversions we've been taking all the sweeter to know that they serve two purposes at once."

Iron then stood up straight and faced Arzades, half-blocking Tempest from view. He rolled his head from side to side, popping sounds like explosions from his neck echoing in the small room. Time seemed to slow down, akin to what happened with the guards in Elard. But this time, Arzades was still moving at a regular pace. He flung himself backwards as Iron lashed out with a meaty paw, trying to catch the young man. Scrambling hard, Arzades fled down the hallway, tumbling down the stairs even as he scrambled his way to the front door, Tempest's soft laughter following him the whole way.

As he made it outside he launched himself towards Damarion and rapidly undid the picket for the horses and began leading his horse away.

"What happened in there? I saw them go in and heard a woman's scream. I was just about on my way in when you came tearing out of there like there was a demon chasing you," Damarion claimed, moving fast to keep up with Arzades.

"Tempest burned the woman they brought in with them, all because they saw me in the tavern itself. I should have listened to you and stayed out here," Arzades replied, leading them southward until they found a cross-street that led to the main marketplace. In the marketplace, he saw Tyrielle and Renias standing there casually waiting for Arzades and Damarion to return. As they approached, Arzades took a deep breath of the open air and began to tell his mother the entirety of what happened on their scouting mission.

***

Tyrielle nodded as Arzades' account came to an end. "Come on, we've got our own accommodations to look to now. The gates are closed, they won't be going anywhere before tomorrow morning now, pup. I can't say I'm pleased with you, but I'm not displeased either. You couldn't have known that Iron would recognize you from mere moments in Arvil."

"I know, but I still feel awful. Between being found out and not being able to save that woman – indeed, being the cause of her injury, even indirectly – I'm fairly shaken up."

Tyrielle nodded as her son spoke and they turned to the northwest road and returned to the Dusty Maiden, where they tied off their horses and went back into Lenallee's tavern.

Chapter 22

Lenallee looked up as the quartet turned into her tavern, with a wide grin on her face. A grin that passed when she noticed the telltale signs of stress on their faces. Sweeping out from behind her bar, she approached the group, grabbing Tyrielle by the shoulders.

"Is everything alright, miss? I don't need to thump anyone, do I?" she asked with her deep, booming voice. Tyrielle half-smirked and shook her head.

"No, no thanks, Lenallee, 'thumping' someone wouldn't really help in this situation. However, I did say we'd come back to you if we were looking for accommodations for tonight. And well, here we are."

"Good thing you came back now, then. We've only got the two rooms left, so they'll have to do you for now."

"We'll be leaving before the gates open tomorrow, we're tracking some people and we want to make sure we have their trail before we actually set off out the gates."

"Judging from your demeanor, the young man's expression, and just what I've been able to suss out about you already, miss, these aren't garden variety thugs you're chasing down. So I'll keep you company tomorrow, at least until you leave the city."

"That's not necessary, Lenallee, we're more than capable of taking care of ourselves."

"Perhaps, perhaps not. I won't judge as to that, but what I do know is more hands on the plough means the faster work gets done. So I'll be coming along anyways. The tavern can survive the loss of me for a while – my partner won't steal too much money from me, after all – so I can be gone some days at a time. Indeed, I've been known to go off traveling, looking for some excitement."

Tyrielle sighed in response and nodded, "Very well then, Lenallee. We'll take you with us to pick up the trail, at least. Now, our rooms?" she asked. Lenallee nodded back, grabbed a keyring and led the way up a flight of stairs. The rooms were across the hall from each other, but they presented a different kind of dilemma. One room had two beds, the other only had one. Tyrielle turned to look at the others.

"Renias and I will take the separate beds – he's too big to share, and I'm claiming a woman's privilege to get my own bed. So you'll have to share, boys."

You could hear a pin drop in the wake of that declaration. Arzades shrugged in mostly indifference – the bed seemed large enough, after all – but the look on Damarion's face as he kept slightly turned away from Arzades was somewhere between excited and alarmed. The moment passed and he took control over his expression again, looked to Arzades, and shrugged as well. Arzades looked at him for a few moments with a steady glance before turning into the bedroom and offloading the saddle and all the excess stuff he was carrying. Damarion followed shortly behind and did the same thing, reaching back to take the key proffered from Lenallee. Facing the two, Lenallee looked at Tyrielle and gestured towards the boys with her eyes, which Tyrielle responded to with a shrug as she took the key for their room and began the process of offloading all the kit and gear from the horses. Renias followed suit and was the first to collapse to his bed, followed shortly by all the others.

Lenallee went downstairs after the last door had been closed and went back behind the bar, calling out to her partner – a smallish man came out from a door behind the bar. Clambering up on a stool, he threw his arms around Lenallee, "I heard what you told the lady earlier. So you're going adventuring again, heart?" his mousy voice whispered.

"Yes, my darling, I suppose I am. I don't expect this trip to end with simply tracking them down. Can you make sure my stuff is ready in the morning? And I'll take Daffodil with me if I need a horse, so you'd better make sure he's ready too."

"Of course, anything special you want as well?"

Lenallee paused a moment before answering, "You'd better make sure I have my bow and some arrows. If I don't have enough, hit up a fletcher while we're attending to this tracking down bit she went on about. Grig should be open early enough – the old codger never seems to sleep. And he's probably got the truest arrows anyways."

Her partner nodded and clambered back down off the stool and returned to the back room, leaving Lenallee alone with her thoughts and an array of dirty mugs to clean.

***

Tyrielle woke up first from her common nightmare of the night Myr died and could not return to sleep, so she took the time to polish and whet the nicks and dents on her sword away, taking care not to wake Renias too early, until the sun came over the horizon and lit up the sky. After a few moments of her rummaging around and packing away her stuff, Renias awoke and got himself swiftly ready as well.

"Since Lenallee's coming with us, we'll leave the horses and extra stuff here for now, and pick them up when we drop her off," Tyrielle directed towards Renias.

"Sounds good to me. Should we wake the kids?" Renias replied.

"We'd better."

Renias strode to the door and across the hall, knocking briskly on the door. Momentarily it was opened by Arzades, and Renias could see Damarion getting ready in the background. Nodding satisfactorily, he mentioned, "Don't worry about the kit and tack and such. We'll pick it up on the way out of the city." Arzades nodded, echoed by Damarion a moment later.

And in a moment the quartet departed, met by Lenallee at the base of the stairs. She was dressed in chain armour, augmented with plates in particular parts. On her back, the haft of a large two-handed hammer protruded. Tyrielle looked her up and down appreciatively. "Okay, you're welcome to come along. Clearly you're not a fair-weather adventuring type, which was all I was really worried about. Come on, and let me tell you about the pair of people we're chasing.

They set off through the early morning streets of the city, Tyrielle expounding upon the dangers of Iron and Tempest, their capabilities and the apparent proclivities that Tempest showed in the tavern they were found in, Lenallee nodding on the way. Minutes later, they found themselves in front of the Rotten Hound. Directing the boys to go around the back to check the stables, Tyrielle pushed open the door with the other two closely behind her.

The scene inside was one of slaughter. Blood splashed the walls at irregular intervals, and the bodies laid strewn across the ground, the few that were not bearing the marks of flame and fire damage were showing the signs of large, gashing wounds. Words were scrawled across the back wall of the tavern, and the walls were, intentionally or luckily, free of char marks. The burns that the bodies bore were in patterns of circles and runes, speaking to Tyrielle, "Wards. I'm willing to bet that once this started, they couldn't scream even if they wanted to," she said to the others, moving to the back wall to read the text.

Scrawled in giant crimson – fading to brown – letters, were two words. "Coming, Anderwyn?" in two foot tall lettering. Grimacing, she moved back to the entrance and stepped outside, holding up the young men as they came back from the stables. "There's... a couple of horses back there, mother, but... they've been hacked up. Dead, at least a few hours now," Arzades reported, which Tyrielle nodded to him for.

"That matches with what we found inside. They're all dead. I'm willing to bet they all died shortly after you fled them last night."

"I want to check their room myself, mother. I want to see if..." Arzades trailed off and Tyrielle nodded and gestured for him to go inside.

Without much grace, Arzades took off at a sprint, booking it up the stairs and to the doorway he remembered at the back of the building. Shouldering the door open, he braced himself to see the worst.

What he in fact found was the prostitute curled up in a ball, weeping, the burn mark on her face nearly completely healed, only the faint marks of a burning brand mark the sign that she had been used as bait to draw him in the night only just past. Approaching her, she squeaked and tried to retreat further into the corner.

Pursuing gently, he uttered soothing words, "It's okay, they're gone now. They're gone, they can't hurt you anymore. Come on, let's get you out of here." Longer moments passed before the prostitute nodded and accepted Arzades' hand. Looking now at the burn mark, he saw traces of a design there, of words in a foreign language contained within a circle. Puzzled, but more concerned for the welfare of the woman, he gently helped her to her feet and led her downstairs, persuading her to close her eyes as they crossed the common room and left the tavern to join the others outside.

"She's alive, thank the Twins, the Empty Heaven, and everything else that looks out for us out there," he said to his mother.

Tyrielle nodded and looked to the new woman. Looking at the burn, she frowned slightly. "You say this happened last night to bring you in?

Something's odd here. Should we take her with us, you think, or leave her here with the people that can care for her?"

Moments passed and Lenallee was the first to speak up. "I think we should leave her with her people. If they came from the closest brothel, I know where that is, it's just down this way," she said, leading the way with the low metallic rustle of her armour. The others followed suit, surrounding the woman wordlessly until they reached a new building, a three-storied structure with a large, burly, bearded man out in front of it.

Seeing the woman, the bearded man knocked once on the door, and swiftly a woman dressed in scarlet reds came out.

"Oh, my dearie, what's happened to you?" she spoke in a sweet voice. The woman that the quintet was escorting bit her lip and refused to speak. Beckoning her forward, the woman in scarlet pulled her into an embrace. "Thank you, thank you for bringing her back. When she didn't come back after going out with those two people last night, I feared the worst. Thank you."

The group began to turn away, to head off and prepare themselves once again for the chase and tracking down Iron and Tempest, when the woman they rescued caught Arzades by the sleeve and whispered to him, "My name is Aranelle. Thank you for trying to save me last night," she said before turning and heading into the building, escorted by the woman in red clothing.

Smiling, Arzades turned back to the group, "What?" he asked of their bemused and befuddled expressions.

A chorus of "Oh, nothing," replied to him and they walked swiftly back to the Dusty Maiden. Retrieving their kits from the tavern, they fixed up their mounts, joined by Lenallee mounted on a huge beast of a charger, with a tent and bedroll pack of her own, with a great longbow also strapped to the side of the saddle. Nodding in approval, Tyrielle swung her horse around and led the way to the northwest gate.

As they approached, it was clear that something had happened with the guards. There was double the usual contingent on guard for the morning, and they were examining everyone coming into the city with far more than their due diligence. They pulled up next to the sole guard talking to people leaving the city. After the perfunctory inquiries, Tyrielle asked, "So, what's got the city so up in arms? It was quiet here yesterday."

"Ah, ma'am, don't you worry about that. Just a couple of rapscallions fleeing the city, forcing the guards to open the gates for them in the middle of the night," the guard replied.

Tyrielle looked to the others and nodded, turning back to the guard to offer thanks before setting off at a canter to begin the chase of Iron and Tempest once more, but with a fifth member to their adventure in tow.

Chapter 23

The road to Mereketh was not much more exciting than the road between Elard and Isolis, consisting much of the same kind of agricultural land as on the other side. Tyrielle led the way, Renias close behind her, then the two young men, and Lenallee at the back of the group. Every once in a while, whenever she could get a word in edgewise, Lenallee would interject into the middle of Damarion's stories, some of her own.

"So, I was in the army once upon a time, right? Fifth Order of the Isolian Knights, the Vasnayans. We went out to the border to meet the Emperor's army about twelve years back now. Of course, as per usual, we didn't really end up fighting, but one of their units got lost on the way to their rendezvous, so we had a set of unusual guests for dinner the one night. There was a brief skirmish, before they figured out it was just them against the massed armies of the Crosslands, and they sued for peace. Since the fighting was over before dinner, we invited them into our camp – disarmed of course."

"Met some interesting folks that night. Don't remember their names any more, but we set up an arm-wrestling tournament that night. I walked away with the prize, beating the top contenders from both armies. Some of them seemed irked that a woman beat them, but they didn't raise any fuss. Then, in the morning, we ransomed them back to their army for a pittance, sending them home complete with arms and armaments. We sent them off with song and drum, then we settled in to wait for the negotiators to do what they always do."

"Couple days passed and we got the news. We were to head on home, the boundary between the two kingdoms had been renegotiated, and the Fifth Order was to be disbanded. So that ended a colourful career in the army, but since I had made sergeant, I had to pay for my gear, but that meant I also got to keep it when I 'retired'."

The others remained respectfully silent while she spoke and for a few moments afterwards. Arzades was the first to utter a sound after Lenallee's speech, "So that explains the weapons and armour, but where did you get that beast of a horse?"

"Oh, Daffodil? He's not a beast," she said, patting Daffodil fondly on the side of the neck, who snorted, "I got him on one of my adventures in the years after my forced retirement. Specifically went to the north to explore some ruins that a friend of a friend had just gotten a license to start excavating. To get me there faster, the same friend paid for the biggest riding horse that could be found in the three southern cities. And, after some things that happened in those ruins, that maybe I'll go into at a different time, I got to keep the horse."

Arzades nodded and whistled appreciatively. "I didn't mean that he was a beast, just that he's easily the biggest horse I've seen. Admittedly, it's a pretty small list of experiences I have, but he's bigger than the draft horses I've seen, even."

"Aye, the bastard did well enough in finding this horse for me," she replied with some bitterness, before brightening up with a smile, "But enough of that. Youngster, care to grace us with a song?"

Damarion grinned and coughed to clear his throat before belting out another soldier's song, one about a lovelorn soldier missing the girl he was courting, only to come home and find out she had married another. Arzades grinned as he listened to the song and, otherwise, the group rode on in silence – it was three days to Mereketh.

***

The last night before reaching Mereketh, Arzades called a break to the regular dueling he endured, either from Damarion or his mother, and simply sat and enjoyed the evening and as much of the silence as there was. The meal passed uneventfully, though enjoyed. Lenallee prepared the meal, and clearly she was as skilled a cook as anything else. The only other sound was Damarion whistling the same tune he had sung earlier, as he set up their tent and bedrolls for sleep.

Tyrielle broke the silence first. "Lenallee, you know a little bit about how dangerous these two are. I'm sure you guessed that one of them was a mage – in fact, they both are, though the big one tends towards the physical from what we've seen. We don't have a terribly refined strategy, but for what we do have, we'd like you to assist Renias in keeping the big one occupied while the rest of us take out the small one, Tempest. We're trying to chase them down before they make it back to the Western Empire, as we will have no idea where they'll go once they make it there and we'll lose them. Our best suspicions have them traveling through Mereketh and the Free Cities. If we're lucky, we'll catch up to them before we make Freeman's Post. And then we'll have put paid to this whole mess."

The others nodded in agreement before she continued, "But for now, we'll call it a night and get going as early as we can in the morning. Iron and Tempest are likely in the city already, and will be leaving equally early, if not in the middle of the night again."

Everyone else bedded down for the night, leaving Tyrielle up with Arzades. The silence passed for most of an hour before Tyrielle spoke up, "Pup, you should get off to bed as well. I can take the first watch alone easily enough."

Arzades started as if surprised by being spoken to. "I'm sorry, mother. I'm just thinking about... something," he said quietly, looking around as if expecting to be overheard.

Tyrielle got up and moved beside her son and sat down, pulling him into a close hug. "I know I haven't been much of a matronly figure to you over our lives, but I'd like to think you can still tell me anything you'd like to or need to," she said, ruffling up her son's hair.

Arzades chuckled and shied away from his mother's touch, before calming back down, looking into the fire with an expression that was a mix of a smile and a perturbed frown. Eventually, when the fire had worn down a small bit, he spoke, "So, it was the inn in Isolis. Damarion and I ended up sharing the bed and we went to bed perfectly fine, but I woke up in the middle of the night to him wrapped around me. I didn't want to say anything just from that, but it's happened again since then, just last night in fact."

Tyrielle remained silent for a moment. The fire crackled and spat out sparks that caused both of them to jump somewhat, before she finally spoke. "So, what's the problem here? Are you not interested in his attentions? If that's so, all you really need to do is say something, pup. Or I can say something if you want, but it would really be better coming from you."

"No, no, definitely not mother. No, I'm asking for advice, basically. Like, how do I tell him I'm okay with the attention?"

Tyrielle grinned widely at that. "My son with his first crush. I'm touched," she said, chuckling softly at Arzades' deep blush. "Just tell him, is the best way I've found, pup. You can tell him slow or tell him fast, but tell him before it's too late and something happens. Speaking of telling him fast, that's how I got your father. I didn't mess around with letters or the traditional courtship rituals. After I found out he was interested, I walked up to him, grabbed him by his lapels, and kissed him. Same thing can work here."

Arzades coughed slightly at his mother's candid response, working to clear his throat. "I uhh... don't think I'll take that particular approach, mother. But thank you for the suggestions, for the advice, and most of all, for listening to me."

"Of course, pup. Always will. I won't always do what you say, but I promise you I'll always listen. Now get you off to bed," Tyrielle ordered. Arzades stood up and dusted himself off before crawling into the tent with Damarion and curling up to sleep. As soon as the tent flap fell closed, there was a soft rustle from the third tent and Lenallee stuck her head out, looked to Tyrielle and to Arzades' tent and back, before grinning and winking slowly and returning into her tent. Tyrielle laughed softly at that and turned back to the fire, stirring it and feeding more fuel into it before she stood up and walked around the camp, unwilling to spend more time near the fire than was necessary.

***

The next morning, they broke camp in silence. Tyrielle took charge of the food preparation that morning, earning a shaking head from Lenallee and remarks from all the others. "I have to say that I agree with them, mother. Lenallee's food was just better," Arzades commented, earning a level stare from Tyrielle in exchange.

"Well, fine then. Next time you all can fend for yourselves, as far as I'm concerned," she proclaimed, causing the others to chuckle softly as they put away the last of the things and mounted up on their horses. Tyrielle led the way off, with Renias and Lenallee behind her, and Arzades and Damarion in the back. Tyrielle looked back to check on the train and grinned as she saw Damarion and Arzades both studiously looking anywhere but at each other. Flicking the reins, she set the horse to cantering, causing the others to follow suit.

As they drew close to the south gate of Mereketh, they realized that the guards were on high alert. "Everyone stay calm and let me do the talking until we figure out what's gone on," Tyrielle told the others. Nodding, they stayed close and followed her up to the gatehouse where a platoon of guards stood watch.

After the initial inquiries were made, they dismounted and allowed the guards to search their packs, looking for secret weapons and contraband of any kind. None found, they were waved through into the city. Hesitant to ask the guards any questions, Tyrielle pulled up beside the first open business she saw and dismounted. She waved the others to stay put and entered the establishment, a cooper's warehouse for the most part it seemed.

"Hello? I've got some questions I'd like to ask you," Tyrielle called out. A muffled response came from the back of the building and a middle-aged man, rough beard on his face, came out after a moment's wait.

"Yes? Can I help you?" the man said in a thickly accented voice, the accent drawing out all the vowel sounds of his words.

"Yes, this is my first time back to the city in a few years now, and I definitely don't remember getting in to be this difficult. Was there something that happened or something?"

"Ahhh, yes. Something happened. Pair of people on horseback came tearing through the gates and came into the city late last night. They went into hiding, until first thing this morning, they tore out the west gate and left again. Since then, the guards have been on high alert."

"Thank you so much!" Tyrielle shouted as she flicked a silver coin through the air and took off running, dodging the various barrels in the way as she came out of the building and mounted her horse at a run. "Come on, we're only a couple of hours behind them at most – they are why all the guards are on alert. We might be able to catch them tonight."

Setting off at a gallop, they charged through the city streets, making their way to the western gate and the pathway to their goal. The hooves of their horses clopped across the cobblestones of the trade city, and they found themselves before the west gate in short order. A cursory inspection past, they were released, and they set off into the western expanse between Mereketh and the Free City of Freeman's Post.

Chapter 24 - Third Interlude

 Two middle-aged men sat in the top of a tower – the highest tower in the entire fortress as it turned out – but they sat alone. One sat with black hair, cropped fairly short and spiky, the other with much longer silvery-grey hair. Between them a game board with pieces of four colours on it. They took turns manipulating pieces of two colours, but only those two colours – the other two were immobile, mere obstacles to be contended with. Every once in a while, one of the players would move a colour that was not theirs off the board.

 Eventually, one of them spoke words. "Do you think he's found her, yet? It's been most of a month," he said, with a gravelly voice.

 The other spoke with a breathy air to his voice, "Doesn't matter if he has or not, we don't have the time to wait for them. The others are amassing forces to *his* call."

Silence fell once more between them. As the time passed and they kept playing their game, and if you measured success by the number of pieces of their respective colours on the board, then the one who looked older was definitely in the lead. But the man with the short black hair never surrendered, continued struggling as his pieces slowly dwindled.

"If that's true, then we probably still have a month while they gather their forces together for a concerted strike. My domain isn't so weak as to fold that quickly, even from the border inwards. Between the main forces I have at my disposal, the militias that can be raised, and the mercenaries I can call upon from the Free Cities, we stand an easy chance against most of their forces. I say most, but, you know the critical deficiency our forces have," the older man said, leaning back in his easy chair for a moment.

The man with the spiky hair nodded, lifting a piece from the dead on his side of the board. The piece was carved to resemble a robed figure, face completely obscured from sight. Both arms were outstretched, and the hands painted so as to seem to glow.

"Mages. We have basically none, and the ones we have aren't anything to write home about," he said, rotating the piece in his hand and setting it down in the middle of the board. The older man nodded and leaned forward once more.

"If Skyreach wasn't sworn to neutrality in inter-kingdom disputes, I'd write to them and call upon what's owed from trade deals made eons passed. Then our mage problem would be solved instantly. Instead, I'll have to respect the Academy's wishes and leave them out of our 'petty squabbles' as they would say. And be thankful for that much at least, that they'll stick to their neutrality even if *he* calls upon them himself."

The younger-seeming man nodded his head and flicked his finger to knock over the piece that he had placed central to the board. It wobbled for a moment before it finally fell over and, once it had, he collected it and placed it back amongst the dead pieces on his side of the board. They resumed their game, though it seemed to be coming to a close, even in silence. But the older man began losing more pieces than planned, and pushed for an attack before he was ready. The younger man smiled as both their sides dwindled rapidly until only a few pieces were left.

"Would you like to call it a draw, or pursue this into an unlikeable conclusion?" the older man offered across the table.

The younger man smiled. "I never surrender, you should know that by now. I didn't give up seventeen years ago, I didn't give up when I was friendless and alone, and I won't give up now. Besides, I think I have an honest chance of winning," he decided, made another move and leaned back in his chair. The older man stared at the board for a long moment before he made his move – it was taking him longer and longer to make moves that would not cost him vital pieces. Every piece was vital when you were broken down to the merest dregs of your forces, regardless of power and presence.

"I think you might just, at that. I don't know where I made my mistake, but somewhere I lost momentum."

Spiky-hair nodded and grinned to his elder. "I can tell you, once the match is over, for sure. But until then, I'll hold on to every advantage at my disposal," he said, which got a chuckle and a nod from the elder man.

"That attitude is part of why – when I knew where you were – I reached out to you to make contact. I needed your stubbornness and thorough doggedness to refuse to give up. I knew from seventeen years back that it would be useful someday. It just took almost twelve years to track you down."

"Well, it's not exactly like I was universally welcome anywhere after what my brother did, and what I did. So of course I went into hiding. If I hadn't been still committed to the cause, I doubt you'd have ever found me, even then."

The older man chuckled and nodded, and gestured for the younger to take his turn. The younger man leaned forward and moved a piece almost casually. The older, grey-haired man reached forward to move a piece before pausing. "This is a trap. If I take that piece, I lose whatever I take it with. This is what I fell for before," he said, eliciting a chuckle from the younger man.

"It's worse than that, my friend. If you look further at the board, you'll realize you're already in the trap, waiting for the jaws to close. Taking that piece is the least of terrible options you have," the black-haired man explained, causing the elder man to curse softly. He reached forward and lifted the piece closest to him, this one obviously female and one marked with runes, holding a scepter to the sky. Examining the craftsmanship for a moment, he tossed the piece to his opponent and nodded.

"You might not surrender but I have depths to which I can retreat to if I'm forced to surrender on any given day," he said, leaning back and lifting a cup of wine that had been sitting idly by. The other man leaned far forward and placed the piece back on the board, but facing in reverse, before tipping it gently over.

"I might be merciless and rabid in defeat, but I am kind and forgiving in victory. Lessons I was taught before everything went wrong. Besides, if you surrender now, you abandon your son to whatever fate has in store for him."

The older man nodded and stood his playing piece back up. "Very well then, we'll try it your way this time, and see where it gets us."

So they resumed playing their game in a fortress on a coast, a fierce sea-breeze blowing into the room from the outside, pondering their moves in the game, their moves in life, and whether or not a wayward son had found his objective and would make it home in time.

Chapter 25

In order to preserve the integrity of the horses, they did not keep the gallop up for the entire day. They galloped for the better part of an hour, then walked the horses for an hour, then cantered for an hour and walked another hour. This pattern continued well into the evening and when it finally became too dark to see the road with any reliability, even by the light of the full moon, they pulled off to the side of the road at a likely-seeming grove. The grove came complete with a small river running through it, and there is where they set up camp for the night. Damarion and Arzades squared off for a now-common duel during the evenings, whilst the other three arranged the camp and Lenallee took to cooking the meal for the evening.

The ringing of sword strikes permeated the evening air and it continued until the food was done being prepared. The two young men nearly fell over each other as they came to the fire to get Lenallee's cooking, earning a small grumble from Tyrielle, but no more than that. Renias wandered the edges of the night with his food, looking into the darkness. Finally, Tyrielle spoke, mocking, "Sixteen years with my cooking and you never complained once. Suddenly now it's worth complaining about?"

"Well, yes. If you don't know any better, you don't know to complain, do you?" Arzades responded sardonically, grinning back at his mother.

"Pup, I swear, you just want a thrashing some days. Am I going to have to take your lessons in my own hand again?"

Arzades swallowed hard before grinning again. "I'm running out of tricks to best you, mother, so I think I'll retire with a winning record," he said, causing Tyrielle to snort and shake her head.

"You and Damarion seem to be doing just fine hacking away at each other, for all that your sword wasn't really made for the kind of fencing we're doing. And it's better for you to have someone nearer your own skill level to force you both to constantly get better, as opposed to constantly getting shut down by someone better."

Arzades started for a moment at that statement, a look flickering to Damarion before back down to his food, unnoticed. Damarion, for his part, simply sat there, eating his food, undisturbed by anything. Tyrielle flashed a quick grin before she finished what was left of her food.

"Tomorrow we might catch up with them, so everyone should get a thorough night's sleep. Boys, I leave it up to you as to who has the first watch. But I'm for turning in early, myself," she said, standing up and moving through a stretching routine before slipping into her and Renias' tent.

Renias came back to the campfire and cleared his throat before speaking, "Keep a good eye out, tonight. Bandits love this last stretch between Mereketh and Freeman's Post, always have. This is where I spent half of my conscription, chasing bandits down out here. And I see a couple of campfires out there on the horizon. One might be our quarry, but that leaves any others as random troublemakers."

"Got it. I'll make sure to keep an eye on those fires especially, and a good ear turned towards the night," Arzades responded as he finished his meal, setting his plate with the others. Renias nodded and climbed into the tent with Tyrielle. Lenallee came back into the firelight then, having left at some point during the discussion with Tyrielle, with a bucket of water in tow. Sitting down next to the boys, she lifted the plates and began cleaning them one by one.

"Best to clean them while any mess is still fresh. For one, it's much easier to do that way. For two, it's healthier – you can catch strange diseases by mixing too much in the way of old food and new food together. So always clean up as soon as you can," she rumbled deeply as she swiftly polished the clay plates clean and then attended to the cooking utensils.

"Why haven't you cleaned them before now, then?" Damarion asked, curious. She tapped the bucket of water with her foot.

"Haven't had access to extra water, which is kind of necessary to the whole process, boy. Now that we do, I plan on filling up waterskins tomorrow and cleaning the dishes tonight," she replied.

The night grew quiet, with only the sounds of the fire and Lenallee's cleaning filling the emptiness. The light swishing sound of the rag on a clay plate provided a soothing manufactured sound to go with the silence of the night and the snapping crackle of the fire. Finally, Lenallee finished up to her satisfaction and stood up, dusting herself off. "Good night, boys. Watch well,"

Mumbling assurances, the boys sent Lenallee off to her tent and sat enjoying the night themselves in silence. The fire popped, sending a shower of sparks off into the night sky, and Arzades looked up to watch it fall and disappear.

"You'd better off and get to bed, Damarion. I'll stay up and take the first watch, let you sleep some, yourself," Arzades stated, rubbing his face with the back of one hand.

Damarion stood up and turned to head into the tent, but paused in consideration before coming back to the fire. Arzades stared into the fire while Damarion returned, mostly unconcerned as Damarion spoke, "Farm boy... I mean, Arzades, can I ask you something?"

Arzades looked up in a mixture of puzzlement and alarm as he took in Damarion's demeanor. A million possibilities whirled through his head in the space of a few moments, before he realized he had not yet responded and the seconds were dragging onward. "Hmm? Oh. Oh yes, of course. I'd think you wouldn't have to ask that – we've been crammed together for a week and change now, you can ask me anything," he answered, amazed at the lack of a stammer in his voice.

Damarion sat back down, next to Arzades and the fire and stared into the fire for a long moment. It seemed as though he was not even blinking as he stared at the red and yellow hues of the flames. Finally, he took a deep breath in and turned to look at Arzades, "I don't know how to be comfortable about this, how to be sly or coy or anything like that, so I'll just come out and say it. I..." he started, pausing to swallow hard before continuing. "If you're not, it's okay, you don't have to say anything, and we can just forget this night happened and keep on going after Iron and Tempest like nothing did happen."

Arzades paused, mostly in confusion, tempered with some bemusement, imagining what his mother would have to say to all this. "You haven't actually said or asked anything yet, noble scion," he teased, turning to look back at the fire to hide his true expression of a blushing grin.

"Are... you interested in me at all?" Damarion asked in a rush, biting his tongue in the rapidity of his question and cursing softly as he did, wincing in pain and turning away, unwilling to actually look at Arzades now that the question was out in the open.

"So that was it, then. You were all worried that I wouldn't return your interest that you had to come out and directly ask me, then?" Arzades asked, a flood of relief washing through his system, causing him to relax in ways he didn't even know were tense.

"Well, do you? I kind of need to know, now that I've asked the question," the reply came quickly, Damarion turning back to look at Arzades.

The million possibilities whirled through his head and faded one by one as they were considered and discarded, until the only ones that were left were the tidbits of advice from his mother that he had gotten just a few nights past. A grin flashed across his face briefly, which Damarion noticed.

"What is it, farm boy?" he asked.

"Oh, nothing, just thinking about some advice I got about a situation like this. Speaking of which..." he trailed off as he grabbed Damarion by the front of his shirt and pulled him forward into a kiss that lasted some seconds before Arzades released the shirt and flashed a smile, "Does that answer your question?"

Damarion sat there stunned for long moments as his brain tried to catch up with what just happened. Licking his lips and clearing his throat, he replied, "I now have other questions. Like, what kind of advice was that?"

Arzades frowned briefly. "Didn't you like it? I mean, it was my first kiss, so I suppose it could have been better, but..."

Damarion shook his head to interrupt Arzades' doubt. "No, no no no. Definitely not. That was plenty good. In fact, it was my first kiss too, for all that I talk a good game. I'm just surprised that *that* was the advice you got to deal with this."

"Well, mother's always been a direct person, and she basically told me that if I was unsure of what to do in this situation, I should just do something. So I did. And, according to her, that's much how she and father met," Arzades responded, grinning again.

"Remind me to thank your mother, for sure. So, we're clear that there's something here, then?"

Arzades laughed softly, looking around the campsite. "If things were any more here, there'd be things physically here, nobleman," he said, amused as Damarion slapped him on the shoulder.

"You know what I mean, farm boy."

"Yes, I know. I just can't help but tease you while I can, before it gets me into trouble."

"Oh I think you're already in trouble. We both are."

Arzades paused to look at Damarion. "Oh?"

Somber now, Damarion chucked an idle stick that he picked up off the ground, into the fire before he spoke again. "We're getting into something, just as we are going to catch up to people that may very well kill some of us. Doesn't strike me as wise at all."

Arzades nodded, remaining in somber silence himself before speaking, "You're right, of course. But that's no reason we can't try to take happiness from the jaws of the future," he replied softly, tossing a stick of his own into the flames.

Minutes passed once more in silence, save for the crackling fire. The two young men sat beside each other, each wordless. Damarion eventually moved closer to Arzades and laid his head on the larger young man's shoulder, causing Arzades to start before settling back down. "You should get to bed, Damarion. We could catch up any time now, and everyone needs to be in their best shape."

Damarion nodded and stood up, moving to beside the tent, when he turned to look at Arzades, "I don't know if it's love yet or not, but it's a good start, farm boy. Good night, and I'll be waiting for your watch to be done."

Arzades nodded a farewell to the other young man and stood up. Looking away from the fire, he allowed his eyes to adjust to the night and looked out into the darkness. Damarion had given him plenty to think about, after all, and when better to think than on a watch, alone? He paced around the camp in growing concentric circles, idly collecting sticks for fuel in the fire as he walked alone with his thoughts.

He thought of a future with Damarion and what that would look like, and what a future without him would look like. And of the two, he vastly preferred the first and what it held. It had been a week only, and only a few minutes since he confessed to the shared feelings they held, but already Arzades felt an indescribable pain at imagining Damarion's death. Shaking his head, he tossed the idle thoughts to the side and continued his watch.

After a few moments, just as Arzades was settling into routine, a snap was heard out in the night. Arzades' head snapped around, his hand sliding to the sword hilt on his belt as he took a step backwards to the campsite, the sticks he had been collecting forgotten. Another rustle was heard, and he caught the glint of metal in the faint camp light. Taking a deep breath, he hollered into the night air, "Awake! Awake the camp! Intruders!"

Chapter 26

Arzades' call rang through the night loud and clear, and as it had only been a short while since the others had laid to rest, they roused swiftly enough as six disheveled men strode into the camp, an assortment of weapons at the ready. Arzades licked his lips as he was confronted by one of the men. The man smelled rank, even from where Arzades stood, and he was armed with a sword similar to Tyrielle's. Arzades found himself frozen in the moment as the man advanced.

***

Tyrielle faced her opponent with significantly more relaxed air than her son. From the looks of things, they were common rabble, likely unskilled and unprepared for any real resistance. Scanning over the campsite, she noted that each person had their own dance partner, except for Renias who had a spare. But that meant nothing here at the end of the day.

Swallowing hard, she swept her sword to the side and launched forward, bringing the sword down in an overhead slash, cursing as it was beaten aside. Sliding to the side, she spun around, leading with the blade in a sideways stab, retreating as it was fended off again. Sizing up her opponent, she looked around to analyze the environment. Seeing nothing, she sighed softly, settling herself in for a game of back-and-forth with this man, presumably a bandit.

***

Lenallee took a look at the bandit facing her, shook her head and lifted her hammer from where it rested next to her tent and took it into a two-handed grip.

"Come on and bring it, then, bandit coward," she called out to her opponent, who lunged at her with a sword. Lenallee backed up a step and swung to the side, bringing her hammer down on the bandit's side. With a great thump, the bandit bounced off the ground and scrambled to the side, spitting blood in short order from what must be several broken ribs, at best. Cursing at Lenallee, the bandit leapt forward again.

Face-first into a swinging hammer. With a sickening crunching noise, the bandit collapsed, face mostly unrecognizable to any who cared to look for him. Turning about, she heard the whistle of an arrow launch into the midst of the fray, finding no target. She looked into the woods, and with very little to guide her hunt, she took off into the small grove of trees, looking for the archer, or possibly worse, archers.

***

Renias faced down with two opponents, his war axe in one hand. A big man, he passively intimidated those that approached him, and these two were no different. One was armed with a short spear, which he used to goad Renias away from them, and the other was armed with a war axe in much poorer repair than Renias'. Every time the spear-wielder thrust forward, Renias knocked the spear aside with a half-hearted swipe. But seeing Arzades frozen and Lenallee having torn into the treeline for some reason, Renias knew he did not have time to play kindly.

The spear-wielding bandit thrust forward again, and this time Renias punished him for it. He weaved to the side, and grabbed onto the spear with his offhand as he smashed the spear to pieces with his axe. Tossing the remnants of the spear aside, he swung once at the axeman, who sensibly ducked out of the way.

Exactly as Renias expected. Sweeping the axe into a two-handed grip, he brought the axe squarely down on the axe-wielder's head, splitting the skull messily before he heaved the body to the side and marched onto the bandit holding the last shards of his spear. Backing up a step, the bandit flung the wreckage of his spear at Renias and turned to flee. Renias tackled him from behind swiftly, hauling him up and holding him from behind with the haft of his axe across the neck.

***

Damarion lifted his sword and turned to see the bandit approaching him to be almost the size of Renias, with the rest of the camp behind him from Damarion's perspective. So he looked to see all the others dealing with their opponents, or not as the case may be. "Great. Of course I get the big one," he calmly stated, throwing aside the scabbard for his sword and lifting the blade into a guard position. The bandit opposing him grinned and raised a hefty looking axe in one hand – Damarion was sure it would have taken him two.

Looking down at his sword, he grinned ruefully. If he even thought about trying to block that axe with his sword, it would be smashed into shards and he would be left defenseless. Evasion was the key today, it seemed. And it could never start too soon, as the man, the bandit, lunged forward, swinging the axe in a huge arc. Damarion leapt backwards and once the axe had passed, lunged forward himself and took a piece out of the bandit with his sword.

The bandit roared in response and kicked Damarion in the chest, shoving him backwards and knocking him over. Scrambling, Damarion worked backwards until he could stand up and move again, this time dodging to the left as the axe came down squarely overhead. Again, he slashed forward, slicing a groove down his opponent's forearm. His opponent's only response was to hold his axe in two hands, and beckoned Damarion forward with a nod of his head.

Inhaling deeply, Damarion paused and considered methods of attacking this beast of a man. The options were either bad or worse. So he shrugged, going for a gamble and swept in low, slashing out at the man's legs, mindful of the position of the axe overhead and skittering to the side when it came crashing down. But he kept moving past the bandit, taking a kick to the side but slashing up the man's far ankle in exchange, causing the man to tumble downwards. Standing, Damarion moved forward, easily avoiding the half-hearted axe swing that was the last desperate attempt of the large bandit, and slashed his sword through the large bandit's throat. Sighing, he heard the whistling sound of an arrow and dove to the ground as a pair of arrows flew over his head.

***

Lenallee strode through the darkness of the woods adjacent to their campsite, stepping quietly as she hunted her quarry. Guided only by the sound of the occasional twang of bowstrings and the erratic whistling of the arrows, she moved as stealthily as she could. She could see the outlines of the people in the camp, but it was much harder to spot the two archers in the darkness of the forest. Slowly she crept around until she approached them from behind.

At the last step from them, a branch cracked under her foot. The two archers whirled around and loosed arrows at her as she launched a charge. One arrow missed completely, but the other slipped off the side of her face, cutting a gouge over her cheekbone. One swing of her hammer flattened out the first archer, and the second pulled a knife and lashed out at her, cutting a second groove in her cheek before she swept her hammer through his legs and then down on his head, cracking his skull. Wincing, she pressed a hand to her cheek and applied pressure to slow the bleeding as she started stalking back towards the camp.

***

Tyrielle's sword rang out again and again against the sword of the bandit she faced. Now that she had more than enough time to analyze her opponent, she realized he was not quite as disheveled as the rest, a little bit cleaner, weapon in a little better condition. Either he was just a recent addition to the bandits, or he took care of himself better than the others. In either case, that made him more of an unknown quantity than the initial assumption.

He slashed out again and Tyrielle knocked his blade aside by the barest margins again. Behind him, she could see the others mostly wrapping up their engagements, with the exception of Arzades who was still backing away from the swordsman facing him. Scowling, she backed up another step, and when the bandit stepped forward to maintain the distance, she launched forward, taking him off guard with a shoulder to the centre of his chest, and as he scrambled to recover his balance, she lunged forward again, skewering him through the chest on her sword.

Wrenching the blade free, she stepped forward, towards where Arzades and his opponent were circling and pursuing each other. Damarion freed himself up at the same time and readied himself to take the man from behind. Wordless, Tyrielle held out a hand to stop him, much to his surprise. He looked on, between mother and son, before watching Arzades with an uneasy sense of alarm.

***

Arzades gulped audibly, pulling free his sword at last. Tangentially aware of the growing audience, he had eyes for his opponent only. Slowly, he tried to deepen his breathing, to calm down, to fight down the nervous impulse that was to run, run away. Get away any direction but here. But slowly the thoughts began to fade as his heartbeat steadied and his breathing evened out. The bandit launched an attack or two that he dodged to the side to get away from. Every motion, the bandit would square himself off again, before launching an attack. This time, it was a trio of sword swings, intended to pin down and limit his dodging options. But instead of sideways dodges, he leapt backwards instead, and when the bandit advanced, he lashed out with a slash that the bandit only barely swept aside.

Then passed a few moments in a blur to Arzades. He launched several attacks that were batted aside, just as the attacks launched in his way were sent sailing off to the side. Arzades already felt tired, realizing that the endless fictional duels of his imagination were just that – fiction. Breathing in deeply, he slowed his breathing to calm down once more.

This time when the bandit advanced, he feinted a slash but instead lunged forward with all his might, catching the bandit off-guard, feeling the sword tip penetrate and slide up behind the man's ribs. Burbling blood, the man slowly collapsed, dragging Arzades down with him. Tyrielle stepped forward then, a single tear to her eye, but a congratulatory clap on the shoulder for her son.

Lenallee stepped back into the camp light then, wincing at the dual cuts along her face, but closing to casual speaking distance with the group before reporting, "There were two more in the woods, that's who was shooting the arrows at us. If there's any more, I didn't see them, didn't hear them. I'd say we're good for the night."

Tyrielle turned to the bandit that Renias held with his axe. "Is that so? Do we have to worry about any more of you?" she asked, poking him in the ribs with her sword.

The man shook his head vigorously. "No, no. You killed Blimm yourself, the young man behind you killed his brother, Big Charp; they were all we had for leaders. There's only four of us left, and we ain't taking a stranger's money to even think about trying this again, mark my words," the bandit said, shaking his head again.

Looking around to the others, Tyrielle gauged the mood. Were she to let the bandit go, there was always the chance that they would come back. If she didn't, then they would be safer, but that might sour the mood of an already dismal attitude this night. Sighing, she motioned to Renias to release him. "Against my better judgment, I'm letting you go back to your friends, in exchange for one thing. You said something about a stranger's money?"

"Oh aye, we were paid to do this, not that it'll do us much good now, most of us are dead, eheh,"

"Let me guess, a slender little thing of a human being and a giant monster of a man paid you or offered to pay you?"

"Aye, that's them alright. 'Twas the smaller one what did all the talking. Big one just whispered to the small one on occasion."

"Alright. One last thing, then, with this new information in mind – where did they say they'd be paying you from?"

"Easy. That's Freeman's Post. We were to visit the Crimson Dragonfly when we had done the deed, and they'd pay the remainder of the fee."

"Excellent. Now run along, before I change my mind and become less than charitable to men that would attack my son and I in our sleep, along with our friends."

With that, the bandit took off loping. There was a momentary pause as he paused to collect a weapon, which he forsook when Tyrielle cleared her throat and he continued his loping run into the dark of night. Tyrielle looked to Lenallee and beckoned her forward. Leaning upwards to peer at her cheek, Tyrielle nodded. "It'll require sewing of course, but it looks clean enough. Come on, get comfortable, I'll stitch you up before we go back to sleep."

Lenallee agreed and sat down near the fire, while Renias dragged the bodies away from the campfire and the young men sat down outside their tent, Damarion holding Arzades' hand. "Are you okay?" he asked earnestly as he wiped first his own sword down and resheathed it, before doing the same with Arzades' blade.

"Is... it always like that?" Arzades asked, breathing deeply and slowly. Damarion nodded before replying.

"It's been like that every time for me. Pants-wetting terror. You just learn to function despite that, because not functioning means all the fears come true, and you don't want that."

Arzades nodded, breathing a further, shuddering breath before he looked Damarion up and down. "Are you okay? Did you get hurt at all?"

"No, mostly just my pride when I risked a lucky attack. That and a kick to the ribs, which hurts, but doesn't seem to have done much more than that."

They sat in silence for a few moments, watching as Renias dragged the bodies aside, watching as Tyrielle sewed closed the cuts in Lenallee's cheek. Watching as the growing night deepened yet further, as Renias passed off a smattering of coins to Tyrielle before returning to their tent. Watched Lenallee return to her tent, leaving the hammer still stained with blood leaning against the tent, and watched Tyrielle clamber into the tent with Renias.

"Come to bed with me, farm boy?" Damarion asked, leaning into the tent and crawling in. Arzades paused briefly, looking around the camp before nodding and crawling in beside the noble-born son.

Chapter 27

In the morning, they broke their camp up as normal. Arzades did his best to ignore the stacked bodies in the edge of the trees. They were not starting to stink yet, but they were still a visible reminder of what happened the night past. But at the same time, Arzades had to grin at other things that happened the night past.

"That's a fast change in attitude, pup. What's got you so cheerful this morning?" Tyrielle asked her bemused son.

"Oh... nothing really, mother. Just... thinking about things," he replied, straightening up and straightening his face at the same time.

"Nothing, huh? You know, a mother can always tell that something's up with their children. I know I'm not much of a mother, far more of a leader, but even I can still tell that."

"You're more than good enough of a mother for me, so you quit that bemoaning yourself. As for what's up... it's nothing serious, mother, don't worry about that," he answered, continuing to aid in the breaking of camp as Lenallee, cuts still freshly stitched, prepared their morning meal. Tyrielle continued working in silence for much of what remained of striking the camp.

Renias walked by her at one point, quietly whispering, "It's the boys, isn't it?"

"I think so. I think they're an item, now," she whispered back, to which Renias flashed a rueful grin.

"It's really something when your children find someone else. It gives you kind of a satisfaction, and a sense of knowing that someone will be able to care for them in the times that you can't. Everyone's love is a different kind of special. I remember when Marik..." Renias trailed off, a tear coming to his eye before he continued, "I remember when Eillel started meeting with the headman's son. It was a relief, to say the least, knowing that she'd be cared for after Alari and I passed," he paused again, audibly swallowing a knot that had formed in his throat.

Tyrielle clapped him on the shoulder and nodded silently. "Twins willing, I'll never know the same depth of your pain, Renias. When Myr was killed, I went insane for a while. I don't remember much of what happened. If it wasn't for Zarik taking care of me and escorting me through the Free Cities into Ketheria, into the Crosslands, I doubt I'd be here today. But to lose *more* than him, I can't imagine what it's like."

"That's why it's such a relief for you, don't you think that your boy has found someone?" Renias replied, smiling slightly as he loaded up the last of the camp onto the packhorses.

"Yes, I guess so. Though I'm sure he's just as likely to get into trouble with Damarion as he is to be kept out of trouble," she returned, half-smirking.

Renias laughed at that and moved past Tyrielle to grab food from Lenallee, Tyrielle shortly behind. For all the bitter wryness she felt about the cooking situation, she had to admit that Lenallee was indeed the better cook. They ate mostly in silence, and Tyrielle looked around the camp, half-smirking again when she saw how close Damarion and Arzades were sitting, carefully concealing the look behind consuming the last of the soup that Lenallee had prepared.

"Alright, finish up, then pack up everything else and put out the fire. Remember, we could catch up with them at any time now, unless they pushed through the night. Them sending those bandits after us makes me think they're going to push onwards, hard. And so we'll have to push just as hard. We'll gallop for a while, then canter, then walk the horses this time, and walking will be our break, so get the most out of it you can," Tyrielle directed, looking around at the others to see a chorus of nods.

***

Lenallee was the first to stand, swiftly cleaning the dishes and packing them away, before tipping the remaining water in her bucket onto the fire and packing that away too. The others mounted up and, upon Lenallee joining them, set off to rejoin the road and then to take it at a gallop.

The course of the next few days passed mostly uneventfully, but on one day, they pulled up to what looked like an abandoned campsite. Unlike most of these they had passed so far, this one still had some smoke rising from the campfire.

It also had a dead horse.

The party dismounted and began inspecting the campsite for clues. Lenallee and Damarion took to examining the horse while Tyrielle and Renias searched the campsite for signs. Arzades occupied himself by picketing the horses. Before he went to rejoin the others, he noticed a ring of scorch marks around the campsite.

"Mother! Renias! Over here," he called out, beckoning the over. Pointing out the char marks, Renias started following them one direction while Tyrielle examined them. Pushing aside the grass, it looked like some kind of concentric circle design, repeated in what looked like a great curve. Confirmation to that came shortly as Renias approached from the opposite side he had left.

"It goes completely around," Renias reported. Tyrielle nodded and stood up from her examination.

"It's some kind of ward. Probably something to prevent intruders, or at least wake them up if someone does intrude. Seems to be inactive – probably only worked while they were inside the circle," Tyrielle responded, turning back and heading to the others examining the dead horse.

Lenallee stood up as they approached, nodding to Damarion. "I think the young man's right here. Listen to what he has to say," she said, motioning to Damarion, who stood up and turned to face the others.

"No visible signs that would lead to death, but here's what I'm thinking. This is a draft horse, the likes of which they got for Iron to ride. Draft horses aren't meant for this kind of labour and racing all over the place and that. I'm willing to bet they effectively rode it to death trying to stay ahead of us. Which means, now at least one of them is unmounted, slowing them down considerably," Damarion explained, motioning with his hands as he spoke to the horse and to the direction they were traveling.

Tyrielle nodded and swung to face everyone. "Alright. That means that we can afford to slow down, because we've been risking the same thing happening to our horses. But we won't let up too much. I want to try and catch them before we get to Freeman's Post. If not, then we'll track them down in the city, stay on them, force them to throw the first punch, no matter how risky it is. Otherwise, we'll stick to the plan, such as it is. Everyone understand?" she laid out the plan. Seeing nods from the others, she moved back to the horses with the others and together they remounted, and set off once more to the west.

Damarion pulled his horse up alongside Arzades'. "You ready for this, farm boy?" he called out, grinning widely.

Arzades replied with a smirk, "As much as any of us are, I suspect. We're a motley bunch, aren't we? And we're hunting down a pair of mages, one of whom is powerful and whimsical in their use of magic, the other is possibly the strongest, heartiest human being I have ever seen in my admittedly sheltered life. I've heard the expression 'as healthy as a horse' and I believe they meant Iron when they came up with that."

Damarion chuckled genuinely at Arzades' commentary. "It does seem a bit off, doesn't it? We're a bunch of puppies chasing down two proper hounds. We can only hope that we can take one of them out quickly and then be able to overwhelm the other. Swarm them down, so to speak."

Arzades nodded and the next few miles passed in silence. As afternoon turned into evening, they approached a great bridge over a river about twenty or so feet below. Tyrielle turned to address the group as they rode forward.

"This is the line that marks the border between the Crosslands of Ketheria and the lands controlled by the Free City of Freeman's Post," she said, beginning to explain about the city they were approaching, "the Free City used to be a fishing village until a merchant fled the Western Empire, before it was even an Empire, with all his wealth and set up business in that fishing village."

"That's more than a little ways back," Damarion commented, whistling softly.

"Way back when institutional slavery was still a thing, even. He lured labourers there by promising them shelter from their pursuers and a fair wage until they got their own businesses running. Despite the time that's passed since then, certain protections still remain in place."

"One of the harshest penalties is for violence, though you are allowed to protect yourself. Also, you're strictly speaking not allowed to pursue anyone into the city – so we'll need to be careful on tracking them down. Our one lead is the place the bandit mentioned; the Crimson Dragonfly. It's probably a decoy, but there'll still be information there for us. Foreigners are under harder scrutiny then most native scions of the city. We'll be watched carefully. So, unless they actually attack you, don't respond to them," she called out to the others who collectively nodded. Turning back, she galloped across the bridge, the others following closely behind with the packhorses.

***

The next evening, the walls of Freeman's Post came into view, with faint, hazy outlines of buildings outside the main walls. The quintet slowed their approach so as to not alarm anyone. As they drew closer, they saw the gates close for the night. Tyrielle cursed softly, looking back to the others.

"Looks like one more night of camping or finding ourselves an inn in the outer city, folks. Anyone have any bright ideas?" she asked, half-pursing her lips.

Damarion piped up from beside Arzades. The entire trip, he had barely been more than an arm's reach away from the other young man, even including the fact that they were both on horseback. "I stayed in a place in the outer city when I was here. It's on the west side, though, so we'd better hurry."

With that, Tyrielle upped the pace to a steady canter, determined to reach safe harbour for the night rather than risk camping out so close to where their enemies were. They entered into the outer city portion of Freeman's Post and circumnavigated the city itself until they made it over to the western side of the city. Once there, Damarion took the lead. After a few moments spent orienting himself to where he was, he led them off down a sidestreet until they came to a quiet little inn. The sign called it, 'The Spike and Clam'. Paying the stablehand a silver coin to care for the horses, they went around the front of the building.

Entering into the inn, they found a quiet place, only a handful of patrons, who were sitting in a cluster in a corner, engaged in some game of chance or another. Behind the bar, there was a younger woman cleaning dishes and an older woman leaning on the bar. As the group came in, the older woman looked up and called them over. "Welcome to the Spike," her words slipping together as she spoke, "what can I get you?"

Pausing a moment to parse exactly what had been said, Tyrielle then spoke, bemused by the accent of the seaside dwelling people, "We need rooms, my good lady. At least five beds, though we're not fussed about sharing the rooms."

The older lady paused, scrunching up her face and brushing a hand through greying hair. "Yeah. Yeah, I can get you rooms. Just don't cause no trouble none of you. I can arrange... three rooms with enough beds for you. If any of you are friendlier than others, I can do that even fewer."

Tyrielle looked back towards Arzades and had not yet finished turning when he called out. "No, three should do I think, mother." Smiling, she turned back to the older woman, nodding to her.

"Three will do, my good woman," she replied, nodding.

"Well, did you walk in, or did you have any horses we need to take care of?"

"Yes, we already paid your stablehand to take care of them."

The older woman blinked slowly. "But we don't have a stablehand," she replied, a note of confusion to her voice.

Tyrielle whitened like a sheet. She turned to give an order to the young men, when the older woman chortled with glee. "No no no, don't worry, we have a stablehand, a good honest fellow. That was just a bit of humour that I use to get through my day," the older woman called over, smiling.

Tyrielle rolled her eyes before turning back, breathing deeply to calm herself. "Just... show us to our rooms, if you please," she sighed out, to the sound of further chortling.

Chapter 28

Once they had stored their belongings in their respective rooms, the quintet went down to the common room of the inn, taking up a table in the opposite corner from where the other collective was playing their game. Arzades' curiousity was piqued by the game and his attention kept wandering over towards it, only to be called back to the table by the idle discussion.

"So, do you think you've become a better swordsman now with the practice you've got in against the pup?" Tyrielle asked of Damarion, leaning on the table with both elbows and hands clasped together.

"I can say honestly that I think I have. It's been more ferocious than the dueling I'm used to. If nothing else, it's opened my eyes to a different avenue of doing things. I think I'll at least be a little bit better suited towards dealing with Iron at least. As for coping with Tempest? That I have no idea about. They're more of a mage, much more, and that makes them a mostly unknown quantity," Damarion replied, prompting Arzades' attention to the discussion.

"We know they're willing to sacrifice others for their own goal. The bit with the woman in Isolis shows us that. They also were indiscriminate with their power in Arvil, though less malicious and more... amoral, about that. I think Tempest just doesn't follow any type of creed; they just do what they want," Arzades added. Tyrielle nodded in agreement and called the older lady, the owner of the establishment over.

"We'd like whatever you have for food and drink available right now, my good lady," she requested, to which the wizened lady bowed in reception, moving to the younger woman who was doing the dishes, directed her to pull drinks for the five of them, and then vanished through a loosely swinging door behind the bar. The younger woman took five pewter mugs and filled them from a barrel behind the bar, bringing them over and laying them on the table before collecting payment for both the food and the drink. Turning to the young men, she winked slyly before returning to her place behind the bar and polishing the remaining dishes. Damarion merely raised an eyebrow, turning to look at Arzades, who was blushing. Damarion's eyebrow rose further and a smirk came across his face before he turned back to the table. For his part, Arzades concerned himself with drinking the ale that the barmaid had brought, which only earned him an eyebrow raised from his mother.

"I can't win, it seems," he mumbled under his breath, causing Lenallee beside him to laugh and clap him on the shoulder, before lifting her own mug and draining half of it in a single drink. Renias smiled and Tyrielle half-smirked at that, before the older lady returned with a platter of bowls of a thick, hearty stew. Tyrielle waved her thanks and took a few bites of stew before she started speaking again.

"And pup, do you think you're ready for this? If you're not, you realize we have to leave you behind when we go to face them, right? We can't have you freeze up again, like what happened with the bandits. This isn't a black mark against you – it would be for your own safety and the safety of others that we would have to leave you behind," she laid out.

Arzades paused and nodded, remaining silent and eating from his bowl for a few minutes. Carefully weighing the options and the facts at hand, before he finally spoke, "I think... I think I'd be more capable this time around. I don't think I'll freeze this time. There's so much on the line, and we've come so far. This wouldn't be coming at me by surprise – if anything, we'd be catching them by surprise, and I think that, for pretty clear reasons, would make all the difference."

Tyrielle nodded, reaching across the table and taking her son's hand. "Then we need you all the more, if you're confident that you'll be able to act, we need all the help on hand that we can have. If I could raise an army of mercenaries, I'd take them with us to go after Iron and Tempest. But that's not an option available to us. Short of that, I feel confident that our little posse here, as disparate and desperate as we are, are as good as we're going to get, in order to take them down. In order to prevent them reporting back to the Emperor about mine and my son's existence. In order to prevent a manhunt for us that would surely send both nations into war with each other and prevent a tremendous, meaningless loss of life," she proclaimed softly. The others nodded, except for Arzades, who simply squeezed his mother's hand.

Meal done, they adjourned to their rooms, paired off the same way as usual. Arzades went into his room first, followed by Damarion who closed the door behind him and went to sit on one of the beds, while Arzades sat on the other. "I know we could have simplified things by getting a singular bed, but I don't want other people knowing that we're... a thing, yet," Arzades said, causing Damarion to chuckle.

"Why farm boy, are you embarrassed of me? I'm offended," he drawled, the tone of voice taking any malice that there could have been from the words. Arzades smiled softly and reached across to take Damarion's hand.

"Of course not, nobleman. I'd think you'd be embarrassed of me, being a 'country boy' and all. But no. I just don't think it's their business, and I don't want to have to endure teasing with my first... love, if that's what this is," he replied, kissing Damarion's hand gently before looking him in the face.

Damarion nodded, smiling back at the larger young man. "I think it's a bit early to call it love, for sure, but I'm definitely interested in finding out, Arzades. And I'll make sure the only teasing you have to endure is from me," he said, smile turning into a smirk.

Arzades stood up and kicked off his travelling boots, sitting down on the bed beside Damarion before lying down, joined shortly by the smaller man for sleep.

***

In the morning, they congregated downstairs once more. This time the mood was more sombre, despite the celebrations and proclamations of last night, as today they were set to find Iron and Tempest, going into the city to seek them out. After a brief breaking of bread to start the morning off, they made sure they had their weapons at the ready and set off into the city itself. Coming up to the entrance gate, they were interrogated by the gate guards thoroughly for being such a motley assortment of armed individuals.

Tyrielle explained to the guards, "We're a group looking for employment as mercenaries, and we can't very well get a job as mercenaries if we don't look that part. May we pass?"

The gate guards pondered that over before gesturing to the two young men, "Even them?"

Tyrielle nodded. "They want to be off seeking fortune and glory and be home before dinner, but yes, them too. And the big guy, and the big lady too," she answered.

The two guards conferred with each other for a few moments before turning back to face the group. "Alright, we'll let you pass. You been here before, know the laws?"

Tyrielle nodded. "Unless they've changed in the past few years, I've told them everything I know, we should be good to go," she added, as she got ready to take the step forward into the city. The guards both shook their heads and gestured for the party to pass, waving them on by.

"Stay out of trouble then, and no trouble will come to you from the guards. Be safe. Welcome to Freeman's Post," the guard on the right greeted them as they passed into the city.

Immediately they were struck by the smells of a large city, more amplified in this one. The sickeningly sweet combination of a thousand different scents, both wholesome and not wholesome, mixed with the tangy scent of pervasive lantern oil, was nearly overwhelming. Every once in a while a fresh breeze off the nearby ocean cleansed the air, only for the naturally unnatural scent to return in mere moments. Gradually they found their way to a marketplace, where the predominant good being sold was some variety or another of fish, or fish products; oils, bones, and eggs.

"I've never seen a market that was so devoted to a single thing. Even including the fact that until a few weeks ago, all I had seen was whenever Arvil had a festival day. I'd like to think I'm not that much of an isolated child," Arzades said, bewildered, until Damarion carefully guided his sight up to a sign, proclaiming this the Fish Market.

"Ah. I see," he said, shaking his head while Damarion laughed softly, "Come on, let's ask around, see if we can find the Crimson Dragonfly."

A small old man with a smoking pipe and a flat cap on his head perked up at that. "Looking for the Crimson Dragonfly, are ye? Well, that's easy. You go down to the main square, go south towards the harbour for about... six streets or so, I'd say. It's right there on the left. But you're kind of a motley assortment, ain't ye, looking for a place like that?" he asked, looking at the entire group.

"Oh, we're supposed to be meeting someone there," Tyrielle responded as they began to walk away.

"That's fair, fair. Many people meet up at the Crimson Dragonfly. I just didn't think... you know what? Not my business, is it?" he replied, turning back to his work scaling a fish and deboning it.

Tyrielle half-pursed her lips in thought, before leading the way down the major street, in search of the main marketplace. Arzades looked over to Damarion as they continued walking, and asked, "Do you know what the old fellow meant by that?"

Damarion shook his head. "No idea. Must be a busy place. Especially on the main street down to the harbour. That means a lot in a harbour city. I grew up in one, I should know," he answered.

Arzades hummed for a moment as they walked. He started looking around, matching the motions of his mother and Renias in front of them as they surveyed for Iron and Tempest amidst the crowd that surrounded them. The colours and goods available from storefronts, kiosks, and stalls they passed was incredible to his sensibilities, having effectively never left Arvil. Then they hit the main marketplace in the city and he couldn't help but stare open-mouthed at everything there.

The sheer variety of goods and services advertised in the square was overwhelmed by only one thing; the number of people packed into the square. In a space easily thrice the size of Arvil itself if not more, what must be close to a thousand people milled about on their day to day businesses. Arzades shifted from side to side as people brushed by really closely, the quintet becoming more and more dispersed as they moved through the group over to the southern entrance to the marketplace, where Tyrielle waited for the others to reform. The last to arrive was Arzades who was just floored by what they had gone through – a marketplace far more intense than any they saw in the southern cities of the Crosslands.

Damarion looked and laughed at Arzades' expression, shoulders shaking in mirth. "You look like you got skewered by a unicorn there, farm boy," he teased, grinning when Arzades shot him a look and pushed by him.

"Come on, let's go, pup, everyone," Tyrielle ordered, leading the way south now that they had all rejoined.

The smell of the sea began to overpower the stench of the city as they crested a hill that lay between them and the harbour. Indeed, at the summit of the hill, the city faded into the background of the smell, and Arzades had something else to stare agog at – the vast expanse of the Emeraldsea lay before them.

"It's so... big," he said softly, staring out over the deep bluish-green waters that gave the Emeraldsea its name. Damarion smiled easily and laid his hand on Arzades' shoulder.

"That she is. Was out to sea for a week and never saw land once until we came back home. But she's beautiful and terrifying and all that at once," he said softly, squeezing the shoulder. Tyrielle smiled at the two young men before leading them further onward, Damarion half-dragging Arzades along. Finally, several minutes later, she held up her hand and pointed to the left. A sign, large and obnoxiously coloured in crimson and ruby reds, with the words written underneath 'Crimson Dragonfly'.

Tyrielle turned to approach the building before she slowed down, her head cocked as she stared at something. Renias, right behind her, paused, looked where she was looking, uttering only the word, "Oh."

Damarion stopped and shook his head slightly as he saw the same thing and the last to react was Lenallee who grinned widely, before looking to the young men and back to Tyrielle. "Oh my," she uttered, leaving Arzades confused, even more confused when he saw the red lantern they were staring at hanging over the entrance to the Crimson Dragonfly.

Chapter 29

Tyrielle turned to face the rest of the quintet, sighing audibly. Seeing the looks on everyone's faces, she chose to address the problematic matters first. "Damarion, do you know what that means?" she said, hooking a thumb over her shoulder at the lantern.

"I've *heard* about these places, and well, there was the place back in Isolis, but we didn't go inside," replied the young man, biting his lip when he was done speaking.

Arzades looked back and forth between the two of them, then towards the lantern and back. Raising his eyebrow, he considered the 'place in Isolis' comment, when inspiration struck him.

"Oh, that's what you mean. Oh. Oh you mean this is one of those places?" he asked.

"Yes. Did you not see the red lantern in front of the other place when we returned the young lady... Aranelle I believe she said her name was?"

"To be honest, I was more concerned with her welfare than about the surroundings – I didn't notice much of anything happening."

Damarion turned to look at him while he spoke. "You didn't notice anything else, did you," he stated flatly, before smirking and ruffling the other young man's hair.

Arzades blushed briefly before forcing away Damarion's hand. "Forgive me for being upset about someone who was injured and returning them to the people that she came from," he drawled, drawing a chuckle from the others.

Tyrielle paused, trying to recall laws of the city. "If I recall right, the age of majority is eighteen here, and if that's so, then you two probably won't be allowed in here, after all," she said after a few moments. They moved over to the far side of the street to avoid traffic circling around them.

Damarion paused and looked back across the street to the Crimson Dragonfly. "Why don't we just lie about our ages to get in? Surely we look close enough that it's down to our word about what age we are."

Tyrielle shook her head. "Corruption of the youth is a major crime here. I don't want to take the risk of being charged with the crime and losing all the efforts we've strived for so far. So the three of us will have to go in, make sure our quarry is there or find out where they are and come back out. You two, make yourselves scarce on this side of the street somewhere, ideally where you can have a view of the front of the Crimson Dragonfly."

Damarion and Arzades looked at each other and nodded, vanishing into the one store that stood on the seaward side of the hill they had been descending. Tyrielle looked to Renias and Lenallee, taking a deep breath before speaking, "Well, are you ready for this? This might be a showdown if they force things themselves."

"I think we'll be ready. I don't speak for Renias here, but I don't think there's going to be anything in there I haven't seen before," Lenallee replied, with Renias nodding shortly afterwards.

Tyrielle nodded and led the way back across the street. Taking a deep breath, she opened the door. Through the doorway there was a short hallway which led to a lobby in which there was a collection of couches and a large desk, behind which sat a short, balding man, the light reflecting off a damp scalp from lanterns hanging on the walls. The scent was reminiscent of sweet pastries and dried flowers, and on the couches to the side were a collection of men and women in various states of undress. When the trio of Tyrielle and the other adults stepped into the building, the men and women stood up and approached them, hands outstretched and lightly caressing each of them to varying degrees. Tyrielle shrugged her way past the crowd and approached the desk.

Looking around the room to see five different hallways and two flights of stairs, one up and one down, Tyrielle leaned on the desk and cleared her throat, waiting for the man's attention. He let out a sigh and finished noting something down in a ledger before blowing the ink dry, closing the ledger once he was finished and looked up to her. "Yes. Might I help you? We don't get many like you in here," he said, folding his hands together and putting them on the desk.

"I have some questions for you I'd like to ask," Tyrielle responded.

"You'd like to ask, you say? Then I decline. We aren't in the information business," the man replied, turning to go back to the ledger.

"It's a simple question. What harm could it do?" she asked, an edge of irritation in her voice.

"Oh, quite easily, You could ask a question that someone else doesn't want answered, they come here, and kill me for answering it," he explained, a sarcastic smile on his face.

Tyrielle stared at the man, lips tightening into the beginnings of a scowl. "Listen, just answer my simple question and we can call this whole conversation closed. I don't want to have to get angry," she replied, voice grating.

"Oh, or you'll do something? Please. If you'd seen half of what I'd seen, you'd know how worthless that threat is," he replied, lifting his hand and snapping his fingers once. From a curtained alcove behind the man stepped a larger man, bulky with muscle and armed with an iron club in hand. Tyrielle looked up at the man and smiled.

"I didn't know you catered to people wanting a fight. Alright then. Have it your way," she said, stepping back and drawing her sword.

Behind her, Renias was struggling with three pairs of hands trying to strip him down, shoving one person away only to have them replaced by another. Lenallee open-hand slapped each and every person that approached her trying to disrobe her, but was still effectively blocked from advancing forward by the bodies in between.

The bulky man smirked at the slender, almost elderly woman who had just pulled a sword on him. Advancing, he swung the iron club at her idly, taking advantage of the longer reach he had on her but making only vaguely threatening motions.

Tyrielle, for her part, was having none of it.

Stepping forward, she flicked the tip of her sword against the club, knocking it slightly askew before reversing the sword and slashing backwards through the forearm, cutting through the skin and numbing the club-wielding hand. To follow up, she kicked up as hard as she could between his legs, drawing a gasp of sudden pain from the man, who collapsed to his knees. Once there, she flipped the sword around and smashed him across the temple with the hilt of the sword. He fell to the ground with a heavy thump, unconscious. The whole exchange took less than three seconds.

Sliding her sword back into its sheath, she approached the man behind the desk again and sat on the desk, displacing papers and nudging both ink and ledger aside. The man blinked, suddenly nervous and lacking the bravado he had displayed before. Slowly, Tyrielle pulled her knife from her belt and drove it into the desk between his fingers where they splayed. The crowd of people attempting to sway Renias and Lenallee vanished down different hallways once the violence broke out, so the two were able to rejoin Tyrielle as she began to speak.

"Now, now, where were we? I believe I was going to ask you a question, and you were going to answer it, before we suffered any further hassle," she stated, wedging the knife further into the desk while she spoke.

"Uh... yes, miss. How might we at the Crimson Dragonfly be of service to you?" the man asked, as still as a corpse while he stared at the knife between his fingers.

"So, as I was trying to say before we had our unfortunate unpleasantness, I was going to ask you about your clientele. I am looking for a slender figure of a person and a large bulk of a man, easily more than double the size of your bodyguard there. Are they here, or aren't they?" she asked, carefully biting off her words as she spoke.

"Hmm, yes, I believe they are. They rented a room on our third floor, quite expensive, but comes with all the amenities that we can provide.

And I assure you, that can be quite a lot. They paid for a week's rental and a week's worth of nights of company. Is there anything else I can help you with?"

"Ah, yes. Feel free to tell them the burned witch is in town, and we're just waiting for them to come out and play someday," she stated, turning around and leaving the Crimson Dragonfly, the other two swiftly in tow.

Once outside, they found Damarion and Arzades sitting at a table with three other chairs on the edge of the street. "Hey," Damarion called out, beckoning them over, "We came up with an idea."

When the others approached and Lenallee had sat down, Arzades leaned on the table before he spoke, "I think you'll like this idea, mother. It's pretty good. So, we can't attack first, right? Or we'll be the ones thrown in prison. But we also don't want to let them go, right? So why don't we just sit right here waiting for them, day in and day out? Go back to the inn at night, then come back again and wait for them again. If nothing else, it will start to irritate them, and that's as good as we're going to get for fighting. Without actually fighting them, that is."

Tyrielle thought for a moment and grinned. "That's actually a great idea. And we'll be in plain view if anyone decides to start a fight, so we'll be set legally at least. But where did the table and chairs come from?"

"Oh, we're renting them from the store behind us. Turns out it's a woodcarver's shop where he spends all his time making furniture. When we went in to hide, he demanded we buy up something or get out. That's when Arzades had his idea. We offered to rent the furniture instead with the intent of returning it every day, to rent it again the next morning. He hemmed and hawed about it, but eventually he gave in when we told him we'd pay a quarter of the price of the furniture every day until we were done with it," Damarion explained, gesturing to the one building behind them. Peering through the window they could see a middle-aged man, muscle running to fat on his frame, as he squinted at the two young men. When he realized he was being watched in return, he closed the curtain. Faintly could be heard some grumbling, but it was impossible to tell what was said.

Tyrielle looked at the two young men and grinned. "I guess it's a good thing we actually found them in there, then. Because what would you have done if we came out to say they weren't here?"

"Well, if anyone got suspicious of us as they came by, we were just going to say we came out here to maybe get a glimpse of the pretty people inside. We're of the right age that no-one would question that."

Tyrielle nodded. "You've thought this through. I'm proud of you boys, at that. I like the plan. I think we'll use it. We just need to get something to do for while we're waiting."

Damarion smiled, slipping a rectangular box from a pouch on his belt. "Bold of you to assume that, I, as a nobleman, would not have brought a deck of playing cards."

Tyrielle laughed softly at that, shaking her head. "Why haven't you broken those out before now, boy? We've had some long camp-nights," she said.

Damarion's smile widened further, and he bit his lip before responding. "There's been other distractions," he said, clearing his throat.

Tyrielle's laugh rang through the air loud and clear.

Chapter 30

Once Tyrielle had settled down from her laughter, she took the deck of cards from Damarion and sat down at the table. Renias also sat down, on the far side of the table so as to be able to watch the Crimson Dragonfly. Cracking open the case, she quickly fanned through the deck of cards, counting until she reached the end of the deck. "Excellent, a full deck of cards. What shall we play while we wait?" she asked, shuffling the cards, riffling through the deck while she awaited suggestions.

Silence awaited her from the rest of the party. Smirking, she began dealing the cards out until the deck was exhausted. "Doesn't matter what we play, after all. It's just something to keep us busy while we wait to goad them into a fight. We can make it up as we go along," she said, flicking a card into the centre of the table. Arzades followed suit, encouraging the others to do the same. Once they had all thrown in a card, Tyrielle dragged the pile of cards in the centre to her.

***

A few hours passed by and they had cycled through the deck multiple times. Gradually they had come up with rules for whatever they were playing, so that the deck circulated around between the players as they killed time. Once in a while, passersby would stop and stare at the party as they flicked cards onto the table. Twin glares from Renias and Lenallee would encourage those spectators to move along.

Damarion struggled to keep his face even as he kept flicking glances around the table, every once in a while coming to Arzades, before he would look away swiftly without acknowledging him. Every time, Tyrielle noticed and would look to Arzades to see if he had noticed. Sometimes he had not. Other times, he would blush and make an attempt to hide behind his handful of cards.

Renias looked up at the Crimson Dragonfly and drummed his fingers on the table rapidly. Tyrielle turned around and watched as a slender figure emerged from the Crimson Dragonfly, followed shortly by a large bulk that blocked out the hallway behind them. Tyrielle smiled and waved them over to join them.

"What do you think you're doing?" Tempest hissed softly, arms crossed over their chest.

"Oh, you know, just enjoying the... noon? Yes, the noon time sun in a beautiful seaside city. Why, is there something wrong with that?" Tyrielle replied easily, her mood settling the others off their edges of nerves, "If you ask me, you could use some more sun yourself, you young thing. You're far too pale. Though I hear sometimes they like that in places like this. Have you been earning much?"

Tempest blinked, their face looking as if they had been skewered as much as anything. Arzades hid a grin while the others looked on. Tempest recovered and composed themselves, before speaking, "I don't know what you're up to, but it won't matter. You and your ragtag band of misfits here," they said, sweeping an arm and gesturing to the others at the table, "can't take us on. Can't stop us. Just go home and wallow in the mud and filth until the Emperor comes for you. And for your boy there." With that, Tempest gestured first at Arzades, then when they turned away to Iron, gestured down the street. The two siblings began to stride down the street, occasionally turning to glance at the table of 'misfits' before righting themselves and wandering towards the sea.

Tyrielle stared at them as they left, watching them like a hawk. Once they had gotten a certain distance away, she gestured to the two young men, "Follow them. It doesn't matter if you're seen or not, but err on the side of caution. We'll stay here and keep an eye for when they come back."

Damarion and Arzades stood up in unison and moved around the table. Damarion backhanded Arzades in the chest and the two of them took off, walking quickly but not running, following after Iron and Tempest. Tyrielle watched her son go as well, before turning back to the table and the 'game' in progress. Renias looked between the two women at the table and nodded, "So, we all know they're together, right?"

Tyrielle and Lenallee both nodded, the latter smirking slightly. "I had to start setting up my tent further away from the boys. I didn't hear anything happening, but I didn't want to hear anything, if you get my drift. Plus, I thought they'd appreciate me respecting their privacy."

Tyrielle laughed softly as she flicked another card into the centre of the table, "I don't care to know details about it, myself. I'm worried that if I know too much, I'll act like a mother out of one of the stories and banish him to a tall, dark tower someplace."

Renias nodded and smiled wistfully and sadly all at once. "I remember what that was like. I raised Eillel to be smart and be able to protect herself if the headman's son, Terth, became abusive, but I still struggled to not threaten the boy every time he came courting. It was less a problem with Marik... but I did joke with his wife about threatening her if she harmed my boy. It was great.

There was this whole scene where we were sitting out in front of my house, me and the two of them. And right when I warned her not to hurt my boy, Alari came out with the big meat cleaver and slammed it into the table we were using," he paused in his storytelling to smile for a moment, before shaking his head. "Seems like a million years ago now."

Tyrielle smiled and clasped the back of the blacksmith's hands. "They were and are good kids, and you keep them alive by telling stories about them, my friend," she said comfortingly, looking the blacksmith in the eyes, "I mean it. Our loved ones live on if we let them, in the stories we tell. It seemed like a far-fetched idea to me, but that's something I learned from Myr. He knew so much from his books and the magic he practiced; some days I wonder if he knew the future even and was just getting us all ready for it," she paused briefly, before half-smirking, "If he knew he was going to die and leave me alone, though, I'll fillet him myself when I see him again."

The others laughed lightly at that, and Tyrielle flicked another card into the middle of the table. The moments passed in silence before Renias turned to Lenallee, asking, "What about you, Lenallee? Do you have any kids, or any terribly sordid moments in your past?"

She laughed deeply, shaking her head. "The saddest day I've had in my life was the day my Order was disbanded, so it's a far cry from anything either of you have experienced. And my partner and I, we can't have children. We thought about adopting some street waif or another, maybe multiple, but we decided to just focus on the Dusty Maiden for now at least. So maybe someday in the future, when the tavern can mostly run itself. Maybe then."

Tyrielle and Renias both nodded to that as Lenallee flicked a card into the pile on the table. "It's a riot, through and through. You spend half the time proud of your kids, half the time panicking about them getting into trouble, and half the time trying to save them from the world. Pick any two you'd like," Tyrielle drawled, with Renias nodding in agreement.

Suddenly, there was an explosion sound coming from the south. A quick glance and the trio were able to see smoke begin rising from what looked like a batch of houses and stores. Then there was a pillar of white light and flame that rose into the sky, erupting forth like steam from a kettle. The three looked at each other, Tyrielle drained as white as a sheet, before they all got up from the table and took off sprinting down the hill towards the commotion.

***

Arzades and Damarion dove for cover behind a corner of a stone building, only to hear the whine of magefire accumulating and then lancing forward, destroying much of the building they hid behind, reducing it to smoking rubble. Scrambling, the two young men ran for the next corner, diving flat just as the next blast of magefire came pouring forth and destroying the next building in line.

"Come out and play, boys. I promise I won't bite much," came the smooth voice of Tempest from somewhere beyond the smoky ruins. Arzades pointed forward and the two scrambled, keeping low as they moved into the next piece of solid cover. Panting softly, they both leaned against the building that now served as their shield, and looked around the corner. Stepping out of the smoke, one hand waving lazily in front of their face and the other held in ready at their side, was Tempest. They whistled sharply as if calling an animal to their side, the animal in this case being Iron, as the huge man approached and turned to watch the approaches from the sides Tempest was facing away from.

"I've got another idea," Damarion said, as he saw the path Tempest was taking near the ruined buildings he had just almost thoroughly destroyed. Arzades nodded to Damarion.

"What do you need me to do?" he asked the other young man.

"I need you to distract them, just for a few moments. Try not to get yourself killed doing this, though. Your mother would kill me, if I didn't beat her to it," Damarion replied, cupping Arzades' cheek in hand before moving around the other side of the building.

Arzades took a deep breath and stepped out into the open street, his sword in hand. "Over here, Tempest," he called out, drawing Tempest and Iron's attention. Hurry up, Damarion, he thought silently, as he faced down the two responsible for upending his life.

Damarion sprinted around the corner of the building, moving quickly until he drew close to the far corner nearer to Iron and Tempest. Then he favoured silence over speed, even as he heard Arzades call out to Tempest. Peeking around the corner, he saw the other young man facing down Tempest in the middle of the street, Iron and Tempest both looking towards Arzades. Nodding satisfactorily, he moved silently across the street and entered the now mostly-ruined building. Hopping up the stairs that were only partially intact, he began examining the upstairs walls until he found what he needed.

Taking a deep breath, he leaned against the stone wall and began pushing with all his might. His shoulder hurt and the stone wall was not giving, but they had committed to this – if this did not work, he would lose Arzades, and he did not want to think about that. But he used it as fuel and drove himself harder against the wall.

It started to creak. Or was that just his imagination? He did not want to think about anything else, everything else became sublimated to this sole task, knocking over this one stone wall. It creaked again, groaned... and began to topple, taking Damarion with it. The stone cascade poured over Iron and Tempest, the former attempting to shield the latter as the stone fall began. Damarion tumbled down with it, landing hard on the stones and dazing himself.

Arzades ran forward with his sword and raised it to swing at Iron's exposed head, but a hand twitched from under Iron and magefire struck Arzades full in the chest, sending him pinwheeling backwards and slamming into a wall, groggily staring as Iron lifted himself from the rubble, leaving a mostly uninjured Tempest standing beside him. "Naughty naughty boys. Recklessly destroying property and trying to knock a building over onto me. Shame, shame," they said as they advanced on Arzades. Standing over the young man. Iron close behind him, Tempest leveled their hand, smirking. "It's just poor luck for you and bad judgment on your mother's part. You could have stayed home and lived. Now? Well, you'll make for an excellent message to your mother," they said as the black smudge that heralded magefire began to form in the air between them.

Looking past the two to see where Damarion laid on the ground, half behind the pile of rubble that he had just knocked over onto Iron and Tempest. "I hope that's enough," he said out loud, and swiped the Anderwyn sword through the black smudge. The ripping, tearing sound of magefire began to surge as Tempest started, shocked at the disruption. The last thing Arzades saw was a white flash that illuminated through Tempest and Iron down to the bone before the sound of magefire filled his consciousness and hammered him down to the ground.

***

Tyrielle ran around the corner to see three figures in varying degrees of conflagration. One on the ground, unrecognizable and smoking from this distance and one enormous one huddled over a slim figure on the ground. The larger figure stood up straighter as the trio approached, scorched thoroughly but incredibly still able to move. The slim figure – Tempest – stood up and dusted themself off, brushing char from the edges of their clothing. "Thank you, brother. I wasn't really expecting that from a brat, not even one that came from a mage family," they said, smiling.

Tyrielle saw red. She took several steps forward before she remembered herself and took a breath, deep and controlled, trying to function from a place of calm and planning as opposed to a creature fueled by emotion. She was outshone, however, by Renias, who charged forward axe in hand. Iron thrust Tempest aside and drew his own – now charred – axe from his back and caught Renias' swing with the haft.

Tyrielle moved to the side, facing down Tempest, her sword out and fist clenched around the hilt. Lenallee moved up beside Tyrielle, looking at her. Tyrielle turned and gestured towards Iron wordlessly, still not trusting herself to speak. The large woman moved to engage Iron, swinging her hammer to loosen her shoulders. Tyrielle turned to face Tempest and drew her sword. Ten metres, maybe less, laid between them. An insurmountable difference against a mage like Tempest. With each edging step she took forward, Tempest took one back, until he stood with a pile of rubble on one side and the smouldering body on the other. Tyrielle looked down to the figure at the side, and inhaled sharply.

There, at the figure's side, laid a ruined sword, mostly scrap metal now, but the bejeweled hilt of the Anderwyn family sword could still be spotted. Tyrielle let her breath out, slowly, dragging her eyes from the body to look back at Tempest, who grinned as he spoke, trails of smoke still lifting off the edges of his clothing, "You can't blame me for that – he did it to himself. I mean, really, who slashes through magefire while it's still forming? That's just lunacy."

Tyrielle screamed and charged.

***

Renias and Lenallee stood side by side as they stared down Iron. The wordless, huge man, flexed and twisted his grip on his axe, making ready for the fight. Renias was the first to attack, again swinging his axe, only to have it blocked again by Iron's. Lenallee came in from the side swinging wide, but Iron reached out with his free hand and grabbed the hammer by it's haft. He pulled Lenallee in close, grinned at her, then flung her backwards as he twisted his axe and nearly pulled Renias' war axe from his hand.

Renias lifted his axe away and swung it in from the side, only to be blocked again. Strike after strike, Iron parried the axe with his own, constantly shifting on his feet to prevent Lenallee from being able to engage him without going through Renias directly.

Then Iron took the offensive, and it was all Renias could do to avoid those massive axe swings, parrying only once and choosing to evade the rest of the time, quicker on his feet and unwilling to try to withstand a killer blow from Iron a second time. Lenallee was finally able to get in and swing her hammer, but Iron grabbed her by the head and threw the large woman backwards as soon as she approached.

Renias looked to Lenallee, looked to Iron, looked down at himself, and drew a deep breath. The next attack Iron launched, Renias chose not to block. The axeblade sunk deep into his chest, crushing his ribs and instantly making his breath ragged and bloody. But he retaliated anyways, first smashing his axe against the haft of Iron's axe intentionally, smashing the haft into splinters and shards. A reverse sweep of the axe caught Iron by surprise and slashed him across the chest, lodging the axe blade in there solidly even as Renias fell backwards.

***

Lenallee stepped forward to straddle over Renias, and started chanting a battle song, swinging and laying into Iron again and again, bashing him with the handle or the head of the hammer again and again as the larger man retreated backwards, bloody foam forming at his mouth. He turned to look to his sibling and called out, in a childlike tone, far from the expected voice for the size of him, "Tempest, help," before Lenallee took one solid swing at the back of his head, smashing the skull and knocking Iron to the ground. Even still, Iron reached out towards Tempest, faint sounds of weeping coming from him as he left a bloody trail on the ground.

Tempest laughed as Tyrielle charged, lifting his hand and blasting out with magefire. Tyrielle dodged first to one side, then to the other as a second blast followed the first. Then she skittered to the side and tried to slash out at Tempest but had to retreat as more magefire formed to protect them. Then could be heard Iron's voice, calling out to Tempest.

Tempest turned to look to Iron as he called out, rage suffusing their face instantly. The loudest of whines began to form in the air, as Tyrielle fell back, diving behind the cover of rubble, finding Damarion there curled up dazed and only partly conscious. Still the whine grew louder, and Tyrielle called out to Lenallee for her to run. The large woman lifted Renias into her arms and took off running as fast as her limbs and the armour she wore would let her.

The shriek of magefire lancing out sounded throughout the small ruins of houses they found themselves in, as white light filled the sky, magefire launching upwards instead of outwards.
"Anderwyn... you don't know what you've done this day. But I'll make sure you know by the end," came Tempest's voice, tight with imagined rage and vengeance. And then, silence fell.

Tyrielle lifted her head, looking over the rubble. All that remained was the smouldering body of Arzades and the body of Iron, now lying still. Hauling herself over the rubble, she half dragged Damarion with her as she approached Arzades' smoking body. They were joined shortly by Lenallee who held Renias' corpse in her arms, which she laid down beside Arzades. Renias' face bore a gentle smile and a single teardrop in his eye.

But it was Arzades' body that drew Tyrielle's attention. She wept softly, holding onto Damarion for support, who for his own part, stared in shock.

Lenallee was silent, respectful for several moments before she spoke, "We can go after them if you want, make sure to end them finally. It's not right for a child to die before their mother," she said softly, "But the least we can do is put his killer in the ground too."

Tyrielle paused, her mind whirling with thoughts, with rage, before she nodded slowly. "Let me bury him first, then we'll leave for the Western Empire," she replied.

There was a cracking sound, then a dry, raspy voice creaked out, "Don't... you think that... might be a little... premature?" came the voice of Arzades from the smoking, smoldering body. Tyrielle gasped and turned back, lifting her son partially into her arms, squeezing him tightly, eliciting a wince and a groan of pain from Arzades. "Easy there... mother... I....hurt all over. And hey.... nobleman... I see you made... it out intact," he added.

Damarion sniffed and wiped a tear from his face. "You damned farm boy, making me and your mother worry about you like that," he said, smiling.

A dry chuckle followed by a groan of pain was Arzades' only response.

Chapter 31

In the week after the fight in the seaside district of Freeman's Post, Tyrielle and Lenallee faced many questions. Who they were, what they were doing there. Who were the others involved in the fight, and who threw the first blow. Why was there a pair of near-children there, and how did the one survive. Tyrielle faced all the questions, multiple times when Lenallee remained silent, answering them in fashions that would put as favourable a light on the four of them as possible.

In the meantime, Arzades spent most of his time in bed, recovering from the burns, remarkably swiftly even, a fact that did not go unnoticed by the others. Damarion spent most of his time at Arzades' bedside, tending to the injuries where he could, running and fetching things that Arzades needed, like food and drink from time to time. By the time the week was ended, Arzades was easily recognizable again, though part of his hair had burnt away. In an effort to make things seem more intentional, Damarion helped Arzades trim most of the rest of his hair short, save for a long fringe that fell over the side that had not been burned.

Lenallee, when she was not being questioned, made arrangements to have Renias sent back to Arvil using a courier service. It cost the last of Tyrielle's gold and even some of Lenallee's own, but it was where he belonged. The only alternative was burying him facing the sea, where he had participated in a combat he was truly not proud of, and that was unthinkable. Along with the body, she sent a message from Tyrielle explaining the depth of her loss and the unimaginable cost this quest had taken, and that Renias had died well, seeking justice where justice was due.

***

Tyrielle pushed open the door to her son's room, whistling softly as she did. "I know children are supposed to take after their parents, but don't you think this," and she paused to gesture at his body, "is a little extreme?"

Arzades laughed softly, the crackling, dry sound gone from his voice. "I'd say it wasn't intentional, but it was either slash through that dark smudge that his magefire was coming from, or watch myself be blasted into oblivion by the magefire itself. Can't say as I recommend either option, but I thought I'd at least take them with me when I went," he replied, sitting up and wedging himself against the wall, wincing as he moved and stretched the still healing burns.

Tyrielle half-smirked at that, her son mirroring the expression, before she composed herself and grabbed the chair from the room, reversing it and sitting facing Arzades, with Damarion close beside him. "So, I left it until now because I wanted you to be healed when you told me. But you're healing far faster than you should. I'll tell you why after you tell me why you got into a fight when I only wanted you to follow them?"

Arzades looked to Damarion and back to his mother before nodding, "We started off following them, like you said. Keeping partially hidden but making definitely sure not to lose them. When we passed the dockside market, they became belligerent and started pushing people around, shoving them out of the way and such. We approached closer to try and distract them, and it worked."

"They left the market by a side street, taking twists and turns through the alleys. We had to hurry to stay caught up with them, as they were moving fast. But we came around one corner onto a side street instead of an alley and they were there, facing us. Iron drew his war axe, Damarion and I both drew our swords, then Tempest said something like 'Oh, please', and started hurling magefire around."

"They must have destroyed five or six houses in trying to get us in the first little bit. Then Damarion had the idea to throw a rock at Tempest just as they started to rain magefire at us. Well, that didn't do much except throw magefire up into the air. Which I suppose is part of what alerted you, so that worked out for us, I guess. Except for..." he trailed off, thinking of the blacksmith that had been their travelling companion, that had been seeking vengeance or justice for his wife and son.

Tyrielle nodded and clapped her son on the knee, "I know, I'll miss him too, pup. I'd hoped to do this under happier circumstances, but... circumstances are denied us. So, now to why you're healing so fast. This is something I heard from your father, so pay attention."

Arzades leaned forward at that and nodded, still wincing as he moved, but the burns, while fresh, had still mostly healed already. Soon it would be not much more than a sunburn, and then not even that if the course of his healing held true. Tyrielle half-smirked, admitting to herself some jealousy that her son would heal from what still plagued her even to this day. But she shook her head and began to speak.

"Your father, Myr, once explained a great deal about magecraft to me. Not so much as I could teach, but enough that I could understand what was being said if he ever had an excuse to go off and discuss magecraft with someone else. He never did, but the lessons he gave still stuck with me, and so I can pass them on to you."

"One thing is, people who are destined to become mages are exceptionally hard to kill. The energy that goes to producing magefire is still present in the body, even if you don't manifest anything. That energy goes into the body's natural healing cycle and amplifies it, and the amount it's amplified by matches that mage's potential power. I don't know what the scale is like, if that means you'll be very powerful or average at best, but I know it means you have the magecraft potential in you."

"Secondly, a nascent mage generally finds themselves causing small phenomena to happen here and there. And you'd been leaving signs going around the farmstead that you were just waiting to become something. Char marks here and there, gusts of wind on otherwise windless days, diverting our irrigation from time to time."

"Thirdly, and this is completely separate from any thoughts of magery, but you're now seventeen years old. Your birthday passed while you were healing still. I think that's more than old enough for you to make your own decisions. I know we talked some at the beginning of sending you off to learn magecraft while I returned to the Kyrie lands with Damarion to participate in their rebellion. I was initially going to send Renias off with you as escort if the situation permitted, but, that's no longer possible."

"Damarion, Arzades, this is where I ask you; what do you want to do now? We can go and form rebellion. We can go and learn magecraft. We could even return home, if that's what you want," she finished, looking to the two young men.

Arzades looked to Damarion and reached out and held his hand, squeezing for a moment before looking back to his mother, "It sounds useful to have someone on hand that could recover from nearly any injury, but not as useful as having a mage around in a kingdom that actively promotes using mages as tools of the army. I think, regardless of what I want," and he looked to Damarion again before continuing, "that I should go and learn how to use this power, how to channel it and do things with it, before I have to face another mage again; and, maybe the next time I won't have to blow myself up in order to deal with the mage and fail in the attempt, risking the lives of people around me."

Tyrielle nodded and stood up, heading towards the door, "That sounds like a very reasonable plan to me. It may benefit you to note that, despite there being numerous homes destroyed in this fracas, that people were only injured, that no-one was killed. Besides Iron and Renias that is. Some were severely injured, yes, but only injured," she said, looking back to see Arzades with his head on Damarion's shoulder, eyes closed. "Ah well. It doesn't matter too much. We'll wait until he's healed more and then we'll see what we get up to," she finished, closing the door quietly behind her.

***

A week later and Arzades, appearing very sunburnt but otherwise healthy, sat on his horse on top of a hill overlooking Freeman's Post. The road northwards lay beside the hill, and Tyrielle, Damarion, and Lenallee stood with their horses picketed nearby. Damarion had remained more or less silent the whole week leading up to this day.

"Well, I suppose this is it. Any last words to share before I go off to school?" Arzades asked, smirking slightly.

Tyrielle nodded and stepped forward, handing over a letter, the name Corthos Vanton emblazoned on the front, "It may or may not help you, but there is a letter for the Duke of Skyreach. He is also the master of the Academy, so it might benefit you to make his acquaintance on top of just delivering the letter. He is sworn to neutrality in matters regarding the academy, but be careful – he is in all other ways, loyal to the Emperor. He was once a friend to your father, as much as a teacher can be to his student, but that may mean nothing at all."

Arzades nodded and took the letter, slipping it into a pack on the saddle. Damarion was the next to approach. Arzades kissed his own hand, then lowered it to Damarion and caressed the other young man's cheek. "I don't know how long it will take for me to be satisfied with what I'm learning at this Academy, but will you wait for me anyways?" he asked softly.

Damarion smiled wide and nodded, slapping Arzades' knee, "Don't take too long, farm boy. I'll wait for you, wait until the Twins themselves die off, but I don't want to be waiting. Understand?" he said, smile turning to grin.

Arzades laughed and nodded. "I don't want to wait either. But the circumstances dictate otherwise. But it doesn't matter. Soon enough I'll get this Academy stuff out of the way, and then I'll come to join you and mother as fast as possible." Damarion nodded and stood back. Arzades looked over to Lenallee and smiled.

"What about you, Lenallee? What are you going to be up to?"

Lenallee stepped forward and rested a hand on the horse's neck as she looked up to Arzades and cleared her throat. "Well, I suppose I should be going back home to the Dusty Maiden, unless you've got any better ideas for me," she said, grinning.

"Well, I happen to know of this one old bag who can't help but get into trouble despite her best efforts. If you don't mind staying away from home until I can take care of her myself, it would be much appreciated."

Tyrielle mouthed the words, 'old bag' in the background and started scrounging for something to throw at her son, while Lenallee laughed. "Yeah, I can do that for you kid. I mean, young man," she corrected herself, "The Dusty Maiden has known my absences to last several months at a time, so this won't even be all that unusual for me."

Arzades ducked as a rock came sailing through the air at his head and he grinned, looking at the trio he was leaving behind. "It's been something else, that's for sure. And I don't think it would have gone as well as it did with any other group of rogues and scoundrels with us. I love you all, and I'll see you around someday," he said, before turning the horse and moving to join the road north.

Damarion watched him until he was but a speck to the eye before he turned away, face flickering through several emotions at once, before he took a deep breath and grabbed the reins of his horse. Tyrielle turned to look at him, watched him encounter and handle his emotions, before mounting up. The other two followed suit shortly after. "Well then, shall we?" Tyrielle asked, gesturing to the west. Lenallee flicked the reins and moved off a short distance, pausing to wait for the others on the road.

Damarion remained still, his eyes wandering in the direction that Arzades had ridden off in. Tyrielle looked to follow his gaze and smiled. "You want to follow him, don't you?" she asked softly, almost unheard.

Damarion looked back and, after a long pause, nodded. Tyrielle gestured northwards and said, "Why not? Keep him out of trouble for me, and I'll try and save your homeland."

He smiled and bowed as low as he could on the horse. "Thank you. I suppose I can't call you mother yet, but it's definitely a possibility in the future. Thank you, Tyrielle," he said, before turning his horse and flicking the reins and goading the horse into a gallop on the road.

Tyrielle smiled after the young man and rode to join Lenallee on the road and together they began riding westwards. Lenallee looked after Damarion and smiled, pulling in close to Tyrielle. "You realize that every time those two have gone off alone, they've gotten into trouble, right?"

Tyrielle smiled. "Yeah, but they keep getting themselves mostly out of trouble, too. I have to trust that they can keep doing so. If I didn't, I'd go mad bringing my son into a soon-to-be warzone. So I'm hoping that between the two of them, they can avoid some trouble and get out of the rest," she replied as they rode onwards.

"Speaking of trouble, by the way... since we know they're an item, did you happen to give your son 'the talk'? You know, the one that every parent dreads giving their child some day?" Lenallee asked, raising an eyebrow.

Tyrielle shrugged and looked off to the north. "They're intelligent young men. I'm sure they can figure it out."